Elisha R. Potter

Memoir Concerning the French Settlements

and French settlers in the colony of Rhode Island

Elisha R. Potter

Memoir Concerning the French Settlements
and French settlers in the colony of Rhode Island

ISBN/EAN: 9783337380588

Printed in Europe, USA, Canada, Australia, Japan

Cover: Foto ©Andreas Hilbeck / pixelio.de

More available books at **www.hansebooks.com**

MEMOIR

CONCERNING THE

FRENCH SETTLEMENTS

AND

FRENCH SETTLERS

IN THE

COLONY OF RHODE ISLAND.

BY

ELISHA R. POTTER.

Author of the Early History of Narragansett

PROVIDENCE:
SIDNEY S. RIDER
1879.

Sam.ᵗ Bennd

Jthn. Aylesworth   Wᵐ Weaver   Thos Fry

P. Tillinghast.   Samuel Bennet.

Joseph Cory

Matteson 23¾ a.   Elisha Johnson 21 a.

Pardon Tillinghast's Farm.   Joshua Davis 103 a.

D.ᵗ Briggs 100½ a.   108¼ a.   Son of P. Tillinghast 102 a.

William Wanton.

Col. Peter Money   261 a.

Josiah James 193 a.

Hugh Baily.

FRENCH ORCHARD   Spring

Remains of Habitations or Cellars.

Line between Kingstown and East Greenwich

The Great Bog Meadow   Bog Mill Pond near Davis   Davis

BRIGGS CHANEL

Richard Briggs.

Henry Reynolds

Job Manchester

Benja. Nichols.

Line between Kingstown and East Greenwich

Remains of Habitations +++

PRELIMINARY MEMOIR.

Of the numerous French settlements in America, those in Canada, Maine, and some others, probably had their origin in the love of enterprise and adventure. But the motives which produced the settlements in Rhode Island, Massachusetts, and the Southeastern States were, in a great measure, religious. The reformation which took place in the sixteenth century was attended with almost unceasing wars and civil convulsions. The principle of tolerating all religious opinions to the utmost limit consistent with the preservation of public morality and order, was then almost unknown. Religion was regarded by all governments as a part of the machinery of state, and to attack the established church was of course rebellion against the powers that were.

The Lutheran reformation soon spread over Europe. In France the protestants were generally known by the name of Huguenots. The origin of this name is not certainly known.

In 1562 the dissensions between the two religious parties in France had arisen to such a height that an open war broke out between them. The Catholic party for the greater part of the time from the beginning of the troubles until the repeal of the Edict of Nantes and the expulsion of the protestants from France, had the advantage of having all the power of the civil government exerted in their favor. The war continued with more or less violence until 1572, when the leaders of the protestant party having been invited to Paris on pretense of bringing about a general reconciliation, the ever memorable massacre of St. Bartholomew took place. In this massacre seventy thousand protestants, including almost all the leaders of the party, fell victims to the bloody spirit of religious persecution.

The Catholics in France and at Rome celebrated this event with thanksgivings and jubilees, and medals were struck to commemorate their victory.

This massacre took place in the reign of Charles the Ninth, and during the remainder of his reign the conscientious protestants enjoyed no rest. Henry the Third, who was supposed to favor protestantism, was assassinated in 1589. Henry the Fourth succeeded, and quiet was restored to the nation for a time.

Henry the Fourth, who before his coming to the throne of France had been King of Navarre, had been educated a protestant, and was naturally inclined to favor their cause. On his accession, from motives of policy, the greater part of his subjects being attached to the Church of Rome, he made a public profession of the Catholic religion, but he was of too enlarged a mind to lend himself to be the instrument of oppression to any party and to endanger the peace of France and the stability of the government, by a vain endeavor to produce a uniformity of religious opinion.

In the year 1598 he published the celebrated Edict of Nantes, so called from the city of Nantes where it was signed. By this a free toleration was granted to the protestants in matters of religious opinion; the offices of the state were made accessible to them; funds were allowed them for the maintenance of their worship ; and for a further security to them against the malice of their persecuting foes and against any sudden change of policy in the government, certain cities were assigned to them as places of refuge and defence.

The giving to the protestants the control of certain portions of the kingdom seems inconsistent with all modern notions of religious freedom. It may have been justified by the turbulent state of the times. But it laid the foundation of much of the subsequent troubles.

During the whole of this prince's reign the terms of the Edict were faithfully adhered to.   He perished by assassination in 1610, and with him the hopes of the protestants for security in time to come.

During the succeeding reign of Louis the Thirteenth, the Edict of Nantes was several times solemnly reaffirmed, and the confirmation by Louis the Thirteenth, dated March 12, 1615, is especially remarkable for its expressions of liberality and toleration of religious differences.

Had the protestants been governed by wise and moderate councils, their fate might have been different.   But they bitterly assailed Henry the Fourth, for his change of religion, and they suffered themselves to become the victims and tools of ambitious nobles whose only motive was to obtain power in the state for themselves.   The ambition of the nobles to control the government was, for several generations, the source of almost constant civil war, and although religion was generally the pretext, yet it was sometimes merely a pretence, and frequently not unmixed with political motives.   Louis the Thirteenth laid siege to Rochelle, which had become practically almost independent*, and it was compelled to surrender in 1629.   But even then the free exercise of their religion was guaranteed to them by the Edict of Grace, signed by Cardinal Richelieu.†

But the strength of the Huguenots as a party was now broken, and in 1685 Louis the Fourteenth, under the influence of the clergy, repealed the Edict of Nantes.   The open profession of the reformed religion was prohibited, the ministers of the reformed faith compelled to leave the kingdom, and a series of persecutions commenced which drove away from their country a large proportion of the reformed ; in effect, all those who preferred the enjoyment

* Weiss's History of the French Protestant Refugees, i,, 48.
† Weiss's   "   "   "   "   "   i., 48, 50.

of their own religious opinions to compliance with the religion of the state. This was a blow to the prosperity of France from which it was long in recovering. The persecuted fled to England, Holland, Geneva, Brandenburgh and America. The number has been variously estimated; sometimes as high as a million. They were not of the poorer or more ignorant classes of society. They comprised within their ranks a large portion of the wealth, intelligence, and enterprise of the country, and were gladly welcomed by the nations to which they fled, as a valuable acquisition not only to their numbers, but to their intellectual resources and manufacturing industry.

Those who settled at New Rochelle in the State of New York, in New York city, on the James River in Virginia, on the Santee River and in Charleston, South Carolina, came over during the troubles which preceded and followed the revocation of the Edict of Nantes, and from the same motives which prompted the settlements made in Massachusetts and Rhode Island. Among their descendants were many who took an active part in our American Revolution, and who were otherwise distinguished as statesmen or public benefactors. It will suffice to mention the names of Jay, Laurens, Manigault, Marion, and Boudinot.

Within a few years after the repeal of the Edict, the settlement in Massachusetts was made by about thirty French families. They received a grant of ten or twelve thousand acres of land in the township of Oxford, from the proprietors of the township, and there they continued to live and the settlement flourished until about 1696, when, harassed by attacks from the Indians and the settlers, they were scattered over the country. Most of them went to Boston. As they had fled to this country for the sake of religious opinion, it may naturally be supposed that after their arrival here, they would maintain and respect the ordinances of religion.   While at Oxford they maintained a minister of their own sect, and when they had removed to Boston they built and for a long time supported a church in which services were performed in their vernacular tongue.   Here, as elsewhere, they and their descendants were of respectable condition in society, and some have left behind them good and great names which will long be remembered.   For a more particular account of this settlement reference may be made to a very able and learned Essay on the History of the French Protestants, by Rev. Abiel Holmes of Cambridge.*

*Massachusetts Historical Collections, volume xxii.

Left column (West)		East column		
Wm Barbut		Est		MEADOW GROUND
Paul Collin		Bertin d'it Laronde		
Jean Germon		Menardeau		
Dechamps		Galay		
fougere		Ratier		
Grignon		Dauid		
Legaré		Beauchamps		
Robineau		Moize le Brun		

The great Road that leads between the Homalots that leads to the great plains & to the way to Boston

Petter Ayrault		La terre pour l'Eglise		
Magni Junior		La terre pour L'ecolle		
Magni Senior		Le Breton		
Dauid Junior		Le Vigne		
Dauid Senior		Tauerrier		
Chadene		Bouniot		
foretier		Lemoine		
Ezechiel Carré Ministre		Abraum tourtellot		
Louis Alaire		La Veue Colay		
Jamain		Targé Junior		
Russereau		Targé Senior		
Grasilier		Arnaud		
Amian		Lambert		
Lason		Rambert		
Belhair		Coudret		
Milard		Jean Jullien		
Jouet		Ouest		
Renaud				
Le gendre				

THE GREAT RIVER RUNNING TO THE EST.

The great Road running by the river into the woods.

The great Lotts belonging to the Homa Jots.

Salt.

THE FRENCHTOWN SETTLEMENT.

OCTOBER 12, 1686, Richard Wharton, Elisha Hutchinson, and John Saffin, a committee of the so-called Proprietors of the Narragansett Country, made an agreement with Ezechiel Carré, Peter Le Breton, and other French emigrants, for the settlement of a plantation in the Narragansett Country, to be called Newberry, but subsequently the location was changed on account of its remoteness from the shore, and by another agreement, dated November 4, 1686, the proprietors or Bay Purchasers agreed to convey to the emigrants a tract in the township of Rochester,* "above ye Long Meadow Kickameeset about Capt. John fones his house wherein Each Family yt desires it shall have one hundred acres of upland in two Divisions viz A house lott Containing twenty Acres being twenty Rods broad in ye front laid out in due ordr wth Street or high way of Six Rods broad to run between ye sd lotts upon wch they shall front. Secondly yt ye Second division to make Sd hundred acres of upland shall be laid out on ye Western Side of ye Sd house lotts as near as ye Land will bear yt all ye Sd Meadow wth yt wch lieth Adjacent between ye Southern Purchase & a west line yt is to run from John Androes Northern Corner above ye Path shall be divided into one hundred parts each one to have his proportion according to ye quantity of Land he shall take up & Subscrib for yt there shall be laid out for ye Sd Mr. Ezechiel Carré ye pr. sent Minister one hundred and fifty acres of upland & meadow in ye same manner proportionable Gratis to him & his heires forevr & one hundred acres of upland & meadow proportionable to an Orthodox Protes-tant Ministrey & fifty acres of like land towards the main-

*This was the new name given to Kingstown, in June, 1686, by the Government of Dudley, the predecessor of Andros. See Early History of Narragansett, page 106.

tainance of a Protestant School master for ye Town forev^r "

The copy of the agreement is signed by Wharton, Hutchinson, and Saffin, and deeds were to be executed when the terms were complied with. The names of the French settlers who signed the counterpart were probably the same as those which appear on the plat, viz.:

William Barbret	Grasilier
Paul Collin	Amian
Jean Germon	Lafou
Dechamps	Belbair
Fougere	Milard
Grignon	Jouet
Legaré	Renaud
Robineau	Le gendre
Petter Ayrault	Bertin dit Laronde
Magni Junior	Menardeau
Magni Senior	Galay
Dauid Junior	Ratier
Dauid Senior	Dauid
Chadene	Beauchamps
foretier	Moize le Brun
Ezechiel Carré, Ministre	Le Breton
Louis Alaire	La Vigne
Jamain	Tauerrier
Bussereau	Bouniot
Le moine	Arnaud
Abraum tourtellot	Lambert
La Veue Galay	Rambert
Targé Junior	Coudret
Targé Senior	Jean Julien*

*In presenting these names, we have faithfully followed the manuscript copy which has been furnished us from the British State Paper Office, both as to the division of words or the use of capitals. Errors may possibly have arisen in transcribing, but they must have occurred before the document reached us.

It is impossible from the plat to locate the place of settlement exactly, but the tradition in the Mawney family and in the neighborhood points to the Mawney farm and the land around and north of the Briggs corners, so called, as being the site of it. On the northerly part of the Mawney farm in the southeast corner of East Greenwich, is a place by a spring which has always been known as the French orchard. Here are the remains of foundations of cabins or huts, shell banks, etc., and in my youth there were the remains of trees said to have been planted by the French. Whether this was so or not, the place is well identified as having always gone by that name, and the country around it has always been known as Frenchtown. The land is now owned by Robert G. Mawney.

At a place south of the road leading east from the Briggs corners after crossing the river, are also the apparent remains of cellars, or foundations of small houses, where was probably another collection of dwellings, as they would naturally at first build their temporary habitations near each other for mutual assistance and protection.

The highways upon the French plat do not agree with any highways upon the East Greenwich plat, which is the one by which the present titles to land there are held.

Dr. Ayrault in his memorial, says that the English ran two highways through his land, and that Thomas Matteson fenced in a part of it, and Samuel Bennett and William Weaver built upon it, and from the position of these names upon the East Greenwich plat, the probability is that Dr. Ayrault's land was at the Johnson four corners, next north of the Briggs corners.

Dr. Ayrault says that the settlement consisted of forty-five families, and that they soon built twenty-five houses and a church. They had laid out lots for a church and a school and a lot for the minister, Ezechiel Carré. They began to improve their land, then a wilderness of woods and rocks, and seem to have been suffered to remain there without any serious difficulty for several years. When subsequently war broke out between France and England, the French settlers were, by resolution of the General Assembly, of March 3, 1689–90,* allowed to remain unmolested on their taking an oath to comply with the conditions prescribed in the King's Proclamation of War.

In the summer of 1687 the English settlers mowed the grass on the bog meadows, and Governor Andros made an order for the division of it, one-half to the English claimants and the other half to "the French families there, who being strangers and lately settled, and wholly destitute and have no other way to supply themselves."† Dr. Ayrault does not mention this in his memorial.

But about two years after this, more serious troubles began between them and the English inhabitants, which led to the breaking up of the settlement and the removal of nearly all. Dr. Ayrault states that two familes removed to Boston and the rest to New York, but it is well known that the Lemoines (Mawneys) and Targes (Tourgees) remained there, and Dr. Ayrault himself remained in East Greenwich for several years afterwards and finally removed to Newport, and was one of the first promoters of the foundation of the Episcopal Church there.‡

To a person unacquainted with Rhode Island history, it may seem strange that any dissension should arise between the English settlers, many of whom had been driven from Massachusetts on account of their religion, and a number of French settlers who had been obliged to leave their country for the same cause. They were alike, protestants and all, contending for the largest liberty of conscience.

*R. I. Colonial Records, iii., 264.
†Massachusetts Historical Collections, third series, volume vii., 182. Early History Narragansett, 220.
‡See Arnold's Rhode Island, volume i., Appendix G.

But there were land speculators and rings in those days as well as now, and then as now some of the leaders stood high in the church.

The charter of Rhode Island of 1663 had secured to Rhode Island certain limits. But for all the outer borders of their territory they had for many years to contend with Connecticut and Massachusetts. It was not until 1746 that Rhode Island gained possession of the eastern portion of their charter grant ; the western portion, and especially the Narragansett country, was the subject of continual conflict; Rhode Island did not acquire peaceable possession of it until 1707; the boundary was not actually settled until the decision of the King in council in 1728.

This conflict of jurisdiction gave rise to great confusion in claims to lands.

In June and July, 1659, Major Humphrey Atherton and his associates, afterwards known, sometimes as the Atherton company, and again as the Bay Purchasers, purchased from the Indian sachems two large tracts of land, Quidneset and Boston Neck. These were called the northern and southern purchases. They included some of the most valuable lands in the west part of the Colony, both from quality of soil and from their advantageous situation, on Narragansett Bay.

This company consisted at first of Major Humphrey Atherton, of Massachusetts, John Winthrop, Governor of Connecticut, Richard Smith, Sen., and R. Smith, Jr., of Wickford, William Hudson and Amos Richardson, of Boston, and John Tinker, of Nashaway.* Major Atherton had been employed by Massachusetts in negotiating with the Indians, and having been for several years superintendent of the *praying* Indians, he had thus acquired an influence with them. They made offers of land to Roger Williams to in-

* Potter's Early History of Narragansett, 269, 58.

duce him to become one of the company, but he refused
and informed them that their purchases were illegal.* It
will be seen that the company was so formed as to combine
different influences, and included besides persons from
Massachusetts and Connecticut, some from Rhode Island.

Subsequently Wharton, Saffin, Edward Hutchinson, and
others, became interested in the purchases.†

But the trouble about the Frenchtown lands grew out of
another transaction. The commissioners of the United
Colonies had undertaken to impose a fine upon the Indians
in the jurisdiction claimed by Rhode Island, and on non-
payment, had sent a military force and compelled the Narragansett sachems to execute a mortgage, September 29, 1680,
of their whole country to them.‡ The Indians not paying
the fine, the Atherton company paid it for them, and the
sachems made a new mortgage of the whole country to the
company, conditioned to pay the money in six months. On
the expiration of that time two sachems, with some other
Indians, in September, 1662, delivered formal possession by
turf and twig, to the Atherton partners. How much the
Indians knew of the effect of these proceedings may be im-
agined. lt was nothing but a mere farce.

The Rhode Island Legislature afterwards, in 1672, confirmed the Boston Neck and Quidneset purchases,§ but they
never acknowledged the validity of this mortgage. If these
lands were within the limits of the Rhode Island charter, as
they were afterwards decided to be, then all these proceedings were wholly void. The Atherton claim had been re-
jected by Governor Andros, and the Atherton company had
petitioned the English government for a grant of land to

* Roger Williams's Letter to Major Mason. See Early History of
Narragansett, page 162.

† Early History of Narragansett, 269, etc.

‡ Early History of Narragansett, 60, 234.

§ Early History of Narragansett, 214, 77.

include the land they had sold to the French. But it does not appear that they ever obtained it.*

It was under their claim to hold the Narragansett country by this mortgage, that the Atherton company had made the grant to the French settlers in 1686.

Nine years before this time, in October, 1677, the Legislature of Rhode Island had made a grant of this territory and established a township, then and still known as East Greenwich,† and it was platted out to the settlers.‡

These facts are sufficient to enable us to account for the subsequent troubles.

On the 22d of April, 1700, we learn from the Colonial Records§ that a court of enquiry had been held in Kingstown to enquire into a riot there, and that Dr. Ayrault's son Daniel and several Englishmen were fined for participation in it. The General Assembly afterwards set aside a part of the proceedings as illegal. But Dr. Ayrault was tried before the General Court of Tryals at Newport, September 3, 1700, for nuisance and was ordered to open the highways, meaning of course the highways as laid out by the English settlers. Dr. Ayrault says, that they opened the highways through his land in two directions. This fact seems to aid us in identifying the Johnson four-corners, as the location of the land he occupied.

---

* Arnold's Rhode Island, i. 505, 507.

† A resolution of the Rhode Island Legislature to establish the Greenwich settlement had been passed at an earlier date, but in October, 1677, a special grant of the township was made to certain persons by name. Peleg Sanford and Benjamin Speere were appointed to survey it. John Smith, of Newport, was afterwards appointed in place of Speere. In 1700, the original plat being lost, a copy was proved and established by the General Assembly. The plat now in existence bears date 1716, and was made by William Hall, surveyor. R. I. Col. Rec., vol. ii., 574, and vol. iii., 7, 26, 51, 403.

‡ Potter's Early History of Narragansett, pp. 110, 111.

§R. I. Col. Rec., iii., 413. Potter's Early History of Narragansett, 109.

In 1687, a French protestant visited New England, and examined the country with a view to ascertain and report upon its advantages for settlement. Some of his letters were published for the first time in the Bulletin Historique of the Societe de l'Historie du Protestantisme Francais, in February, 1867. They were translated by E. T. Fisher, and published in the Liberal Christian, a newspaper published in New York, and since re-published in a quarto pamphlet, at Brooklyn, New York, in 1868, under the title of "Report of a French Protestant Refugee in Boston, 1687."

He made a visit to the French settlement in Rhode Island, but unfortunately the letter written in December, 1687, in which he gave an account of it, is lost. In another letter, November, 1687, he briefly mentions it thus: "There are at Narragansett about one hundred persons of the faith. M. Carré* is their minister."

This is all the information we can obtain in regard to the settlement. Several families remained in Rhode Island without being disturbed: two families at least in the very neighborhood where the strife occurred: thus showing that the trouble did not grow out of their nationality. In a subsequent part of this memoir, we shall give an account of several of the families of the Frenchtown settlement, and of some other French settlers in Rhode Island.

It is with great difficulty that their descendants can now be traced, so great have been the changes and corruptions of the names. Two or three such have already been noted,

---

*A sermon by M. Carre was printed at Boston in 1689, under the following title, "The charitable Samaritan, a sermon on the tenth chapter of Luke, verses 30-85. Pronounced in the French Church at Boston, by Ezechiel Carre, formerly Minister of Rochechalais, (sic) in France, now Minister of the French Colony on Narrraganset, translated into English, by N. Walter." This title is taken from the Brinley Catalogue. The little volume found its way from the Brinley sale to the Library of Congress.

for instance, Le Moine became Money and still later Mawney; Ganeaux became Gano; Daille became Daily or Daly; Targé became Tourgee.　Many others might be shown, but these suffice to explain the difficulty in following them. Upon the breaking up of the Narragansett settlement, many of the settlers went to the southern states.　Among those who probably thus again emigrated were Pierre Collin, Daniel Jouet, Moyez Le Brun, Daniel Le Gendre, Louis de St. Julien, and Legree.

DOCUMENTS

RELATING TO THE

FRENCH SETTLEMENTS

IN THE

COLONY OF RHODE ISLAND,

FROM THE

BRITISH STATE PAPER OFFICE, LONDON.

THE CONTRACT WITH THE BAY PURCHASERS.

Whereas there was Articles of Agreement made & Concluded Between Richd Wharton Esqr Elisha Hutchinson & John Saffin ye Committee for ye proprietr^s of ye Narraganstt Country and Ezekiell Carré Peter Berton & oth^{rs} french Gentlemen their friends & Associates whose names are thereunto Subscribed Bearing date ye 12th day of Octo^r last Concerning ye Settlement of a Place called Newberry Plantations in ye Narraganstt Country wch upon Second Consideration in regard of ye Remoateness of ye same from ye Sea they have by ye Mutual Consent of ye S^d Committee declined ye Settlement of ye S^d Plantation & ye S^d Master Ezekiell Carré Master Berton in behalfe of themselves & oth^{rs} their friends & Associates who have hereunto Subscribed are now Come to & have made a new Agreem^t In manner and forme following this 4th day of Nouemb^r 1686 Annoq^r R R S Jacobi Secundi Anglia & Secundo Viz

Imprimus That ye S^d Richd Wharton Esqr Capt Elisha Hutchinson & John Saffin ye aforesd Committee do by these Prsents Couenant Grant & Agree to & wth ye S^d Ezekiell Carré Peter Berton French Gentlemen their friends & Associates who have hereunto Subscribed to lay out A meet & Considerable tract of Land in ye Township of Rochester* above ye Long Meadow Kickameeset about Capt John fones his house wherein Each Family y^t desires it shall have one hundred Acres of upland in two Divisions viz A house lott Containing twenty Acres being twenty Rods broad in ye front laid out in due ord^r wth Street or high way of Six Rode broad to run between ye S^d lotts upon wch they shall

*See note, page 13.

front Secondly yt ye Second devission to make ye Sd hundred acres of upland shall be laid out on ye Western Side of ye Sd house lotts as near as ye Land will bear yt all ye Sd Meadow wth yt wch lieth Adjacent between ye Southern Purchase and a west line yt is to run from John Androes Northern Corner above ye Path shall be divided into one hundred parts each one to have his proportion according to ye quantity of Land he shall take up & Subscrib for yt there shall be laid out for ye Sd Mr Ezekiel Carré ye p'sent Minister one hundred & fifty acres of upland & meadow in ye same manner proportionable Gratis to him & his heires forevr & one hundred acres of upland & meadow proportionable to an Orthodox Protestant Ministrey and fifty acres of like land towards the Maintainance of a Protestant Schoolmaster for ye Town forevr yt for Every hundred Acres of Land be it upland or meadow laid out in forme aforeSd each one shall pay pay unto ye Sd Comittee or Assignes twenty pounds in Currant money or in goods answrable to their satisfaction yt those yt are not able to do or se cause at prsent to pay for their Land they shall have three years time for payment at ye rate of twenty-five pounds per hundred acres laid out as aforeSd & So According to Proportion for wt Land they shall take up & Subscribe for & in Case they doe not pay wthin the tearme of three years each one shall pay interest for ye Same at ye rate of Six per cent & for wt money any one shall pay sooner it shall be abated accordingly yt untill ye Sd Meadow be divided those yt inhabit first on ye place in AforeSd Shall have the Benefitt of Improvemt & likewise of ye undivided Lands Adjacent untill they be othrwise disposed yt upon payment of ye money for ye Land as aforeSd & Leagall Deeds shall be Given Signed & Sealed by ye Sd Committee to Each one According to his Proportion of Land Granted in Wittness whereof the Parties

within mentioned have each for themselves Interchangable
Sett their hands & Seales the day and year above written
   Signed Sealed & Delivered
by Mr. Hutchinson & Saffin   Richard Wharton   (.)
   In the presence of   Elisha Hutchinson (.)
Walter Steuen Junr John Saffin   (.)
Lodowick Updick
John Gore
Alexander Huling   A true Coppy Extracted out
                  of ye Originall & Compaired
                  Octor ye 13th in ye year 1692
            By me John Heath Conservat^r
[Indorsed] Coppy of Mr Wharton &c agreem^t with Ezekiell
Carre &c for Settleing a town in the Narraganst

THE COMPLAINT AND REMONSTRANCE

OF

DR. AYRAULT.

The Complaint & Remonstrance of Petter Ayrault In Habitant in ye French Town in Narraganstt of Some Iregularities & Inhumanities Proceed upon him July 23th 1700 by Some of ye Inhabitants of ye Town of East Greenwick in Said Narraganstt Vizt

That upon ye 23th of Sd July, there Came unto my house in Sd French Town after Sun Sett a great number of ye town of Greenwick mixt wth some of Warrwick & Chantecutt who told me yt ye Court on ye othr side ye River wch was keept at ye house of Pardon Tillinghast in Sd Town desired to speak wth me I told them I was unwilling to go, out of my house so late at night who Replyed we have a Warrant & if you will not go fairly we will force you. Upon wch I asked them for a Sight of their warrant & to Read ye same to me wch ye Utterly Refused & putt ye same in their Pocketts notwthstanding I was very Importunate wth them to give me a Coppy of their warrant for my mony wch they absolutely Refused & Instantly laid their hands upon me & dragged me to ye River Side & aftrwards ovr sd river & placed me in their Court as they Called it at yt time of Night where I was Interrogeted by them or most of them of Sd Court my Reply to them was I was a Stranger & Undrstood not English & therefore desired I might have an Interpreter they told me I should have one, on ye Morrow Soe they left me & my Son Danll at liberty upon Samll Bennetts word yt I would answer it Next day wch accordingly I did & Gave bond for my appearance to the next Court lett it be

Considᵣed yᵗ I was Sett upon In my own house at yᵗ Unseasonable time wᵗʰ a Warrant wᶜʰ they were ashamed to read
or give a Coppy of In fine my wife an aged Woman of Sixty
years of Age Infirm & Siok Could not by all her Cryes &
Teares perswade them to Disiste but Contraywise did Strike
& flung hir on yᵉ Pavement.-where she Continued Some
time for dead all wᶜʰ I Conceive is not only UnNaturall &
Inhumaine & against all Law & Reason wᶜʰ I Submit to a
further Determination.

                                             Pierre Ayrault
Augusᵗt 5th 1700

Allso yᵉ Most Notorious & Ill behaviour of Samˡˡ Davis
& Abner Spencer to my Son Daniell Ayrault who they found
at my house yᵉ Same time I was fetcht away & wᵗʰout cause
for yᵉ same they tooke my Sᵈ Son & Puling him out of my
house took by the head Feet carried him along some Part of
the way to said Tillinghast spoken of & flinging down on the
Stones Pulling him a long Giving him no reason for their so
doing and bringing him before their Court so called lett him
goe whose Complaint of Injustice to them no notice was
taken of, thus are we endangered of being ruened & Destroyed by Such lawles persons So I have great cause to seek
releiff therein

                                             Pierre Ayrault
August: 5: 1700.

Newport August: 7: 1700 Doctor Pierre Ayrault appeared
before us whose names are here Under written whose are
Commissionated to hear and Enquire into yᵉ Irregularityes
Cmomitted in yᵉ Colony of Rhode Island & Providᶜᵉ Plantations & Sᵈ Ayrault haveing made his Complaint of Injustice
done him and haveing on the other Leafe Given it Under his

hand did upon his Corporall Oath before us aver it to be ye Reall Truth.

Francis Brinley
Peleg Sanford ⎬ Commissiors
Nath Coddington

[Indorsed.] true Coppy of Pierre Ayrault Complaint of abuse receivd

July 23: 1700.

FURTHER COMPLANT AND REMONSTRANCE

OF

DR. AYRAULT.

May it Please yor Excellency

I Lately made bold to Lay before yor Excellency by Petition Some part of my grivances & wrongs done me on my lands purchased in ye Narraganst^t Country in ye Town of Rochester of ye proprie^{rs} thereof & have here given a short and true Remonstrance of myself & Distressed Country people Settlem^t & ye sever^{ll} Occurances and Passages they & myself past thro there

Upon the fourth day of Nouemb^r 1686 Richard Wharton Esqr &c & on our part our Minist^r Ezekiel Carre & Peter Berton agrees for a Sertain parsell of Land in S^d Narraganst^t Country for Settling A Town thereon of an hundred acres apiece to a family wch was done & Compleated o^r sever^{ll} allotments laid out & a Coppy of ye Articles I make bold to prsent yor Excellency wth, & wth a true Coppy of ye Platt of o^r sever^{ll} Settlem^t & Allotment as Laid out & we was there Settled by ye then Proprie^{rs} & Goverment who gaue us oath of Alleagance we being about forty five five familys building about twenty five houses wth Some Sellars in ye Ground Setting up o^r Church & it being a very wilderness Country fild alltogether wth wood & stones & no former Improvements made thereon y^t o^r Labour charge & trouble was great but we had A Comfort we could then Injoy o^r worship to God & had y^e Governm^{ts} Protection to us in o^r Improvem^{ts} no p^{r}son disturbing us ou our Labour no P$_r$tending any claime to any of y^e soile but they purchases of S^d Lands by whom we were Setled we paying all takes to the

Goverment as was laid on us we peaceable Injoyed our
Lands and Improvements wthout any thing of ye least moles-
tation Under the then Goverment

The then 'Govermt being Removed we was then taken
Undr ye Govermt of ye Colony of Rhode Island &c who
seemed to treat us civelly also at ye first not Molesting us &
upon ye 20 of February 16$\frac{89}{90}$ they Generll Court past an Act
yt we should be Sent for to Warwick by Majr John Green
one of the Assists whereby it should be signified unto us his
Majties Pleasure of an Act of Indulgance unto such french-
men as we, yt we Should be required to take ye Oath of Alleigance to his then prsent Majty wch according to Sd Genll
Court Act we were sent for to Warwick & Gave or oath of
Alleigance & had his Majties Act of Indulgence read to us &
a Promise of our Protection from Sd Govermt Undr or Libertys & Propertys

But the obseruance of Sd Act of Indulgence & ye Protecting of us in or libertys & Propertys wee continued not two
years Undr Sd Govermt before we were molested by ye
Uulgar Sort of they People who flynging down of or fences
laying open our Lands to ruen Soe that all Benefitt thereby
we were Deprived thereof (ruen looked on us in a Dismall
State or wives & children liveing in fear of ye threats of
many unruly prsons) & wt Benefit we Expected from or Lands
for Subsistance was destroyed by Secretly Laying open or
fences by night & day & wt little we had prserued by flying
from france we had laid out undr ye then Improvements
looked so hard upon us to see ye Cryes of or wives & Children Lamenting their sad 'fate flying from Persecution and
Comeing Under his Majesties Gracious Indulgance And by
ye Governmt promised us yet we Ruened & when we Complained to the Govermt we could have no relief altho some
would a helped us we Judge If by their Patience they could
a Born Such Ill Treatments as they must expect to a meet

wth by ye Unruly Inhabitants their Settled also many of ye English Inhabitants Compassionating o^r Condition would a helped us but when they used any means therein they were Evilly treated so y^t these things did put us then upon looking for a place of Shelter in o^r Disstresed Condition & hereing y^t many of o^r Distressed Country people had been protected & well treated in Boston & Yorke some of o^r principale persons went to Boston & York to seek out new Habitations where ye Govermtts had Compassion of them & gave them relief, & help to their wives & Children Subsistance only two familys moveing to Boston & they rest to New York & their bought Lands some of them & had time given them for payment & so was they all forced away from their Lands & houses orchards & vineyards taking some small matter from some English people for somew^t of their Labour thus Leaveing all habitations some people got not anything for their Labour & Improvem^{ts} but Greenwich men who had given us ye disturbance giting on ye Land so Improved in any way they Could & soon demolished & puld down o^r Church.

But I being perswaded by many to stay & haveing fenced in fifty Acres of Land purchased & made very good Improvements by a large Orchard Garden & Uineyard & a good house was willing to keep my Settlement a bear all outrages Comitted Against me wch furth^r shall be related to, and as many p^rsons who in their Sickness and Extremity would send for me to Administer help unto them wch Under God's Goodness I have been a help to raise many from Extream Sickness yet have they soon forgot my Labour & rewarded me wth Endeavours to root me out of my habitations & by flynging down my fences y^t I might not have any Subsistance by my Land these Endeavors not succeeding in all their Endeavours and oth^r Contrivance was against me

Upon the 25 of Jan^r ^{16 95/6} one Giles Pearse & John Smith agreed togeath^r in a Clandistine manner to gitt me out of my habitation & Improvem^{ts} & for y^t end S^d Pearse sells one part of my Land about twenty five Acres to S^d Smith in S^d Deed Containing my houses orchards Gardens & most part of ye best of my Improved Lands & in S^d Deed was allso Comprehended ye habitations to houses & Lands of three oth^r persons then Liveing on S^d Lands this being about tenn years after o^r Settlements & Improvem^{ts} as mentioned S^d deed takeing in Ninety Acres of Lands (as mentioned all w^{thin} fences & Improvements) & ye same day ye deed was Signed and Sealed & ye witnesses spoken to not to Deuvlge their secreed act the same day they went to Greenwich both Smith & Pearse before a Justice of ye Peace one John Heath & acknowledged it to be their act before S^d Justice & ye 27th day of S^d month S^d Justice of ye Peace who had ye records of Greenwich placed S^d deed on record & S^d Justice herein was privy & Knowing to ye S^d Clandistine Acts of S^d Pearse & Smith who certainly knew ye sale of ye Land Und^r w^t Circumstances ye were undr After this S^d Smith & Adherance gave me much trouble & ye rest of us puling down o^r fences & I complained to ye Authority neuer could find relief I Keeping my house y^t ye Could not have any Opportunity to Enter in (to dispossess me & these Actiones not takeing Effect for in my distress many of Neighbours did Comfort me) y^t their would be some relief from ye Crown to me & they Proprie^{rs} of S^d Country & then anoth^r projecet was put in Execution against me for as I have declared Greenwich men at their pleasure Extended their lines* time aft^r time without any

*Dr. Ayrault complains that the English kept encroaching on them. He does not seem to have had the least knowledge that there was a dispute as to the title to the lands. So far from encroaching on them, there is not the least evidence that the bounds of the grant made to the English settlers by the Colony of Rhode Island were ever changed in that neighborhood. Farther east they were changed, and the State Records give the particulars.

authority as I Understand from ye Proprietrs of Sd Country
or ye Genll Court & took in at last all ye French Town &
upon ye 14th of febr $\frac{1699}{1700}$ Greenwich & Severll of ye Town
of Warwick wth a Plat of such a parsell of land wch they
Called Greenwich Township prsents it to ye Generll Assembly ye Assembly Confirms ye Lands comprehended in
Sd Plat to be wthin Greenwich Township wthout Considring
yt Greenwich had Intrenched upon ye othr towns adjoyning
& they haveing ye Jurisdiction soon set to work for my
Ruen in anothr way in wt ye Could

And as I have now Sd & given an accoutt of my Settlmt
fenceing & Improvements & so about fourteen years aftr
upon ye 23 of July 1700 two of ye Assists of Warwick
(viz) Benjn Barton and Benjn Smith came to ye new Township of Greenwich wch had Swallowed up all ye french
Town bringing wth them a number of Warwick & Greenwich men & at ye house of one Pardon Tillinghast one
of ye houses in ye french Town there they held a Court
of Enquiry as they called it one Capt John Fones wth
Severll othrs hereing of Sd Appointed Court came to
Inspect into their Proceedings & Capt John Fones took
an accott thereof of yt days Proceedall whilest he
was their wth his oath given to ye same a true
Coppy Thereof I have allso here laid before yor Excellency also a true Coppy how I was dealt wth yt
Evenin aftr Sun Down how there came to my house
a great Numbr of Greenwich & Warwick people &
wthout shewing me any warrant for wt they
Came for draging me Away to their Court house & ye result
of ye Court ye next day & how by their Plat obtained by
ye Assembly in ye month of February 1699 before past they
sett out two highways to run throughy Land & bound me
in a bond to the next Court wch by ye Govrs Warrant &
othrs Signing wth him afterwards was laid out one of Sd high-

ways on one Side of my Land ye whole Length thereof Run-
ing through my orchard ten Rod in wideth destroying my
orchard part of wch Land one Thos Mattison have since
fenced in & Improves & ye othr highway they ordred to run
athirt my Land takeing away about twenty acres of my
Land ye wch one Samll Bennett & Wm Weaver have built
thereon & Improves Sd Land so yt of my fifty Acres I haue
about twenty Acres left me & ye (known highway) or Road
into ye Country yt allways was & lay on ye othr Side of
my Sd Land since Sd Action ye Widow Smith widow of
ye Sd John Smith herein mentioned have fenced in every
part thereof setting a house on Part of Sd highway & no
notice taken thereof thus I can but in a Brief give yor Excellency a short Accott of Part of my trouble & Pray all Endeavours may be used to give Relief to your Distressed &
most Humble Seruant

Pierre Ayrault

Greenwich August 20: 1705.

[Indorsed.] Doctor Ayrault remonstrance of his Troubles.

Narrag:st   Att a Court held at ye House of Pardon Tillinghast att ye French Town or Plantation so called in Kings
Province July 23 1700.

Present.

Mr Benjn Barton Assist
Mr Benjn Smith Assist
Mr John Spencer Justice
Mr John Heath Clerke
Mr Thomas Fry Attorney
    The Jury returned but not by the Sheriff (viz)
Mr Peter Greene Foreman
Mr Benjn Greene
Mr Jabesh Greene
Mr Amos Stafford
Mr Jeremiah Westcot
Mr Othenell Gorton
Mr Samll Gorton Junr
Mr Charles Holdon
Mr Joseph Stafford
Mr John Potter
Mr John Burton
Mr Thos Burlingham
    The Court being Sate ye Jury was called to take their
Engagements which was Administred unto them (but not
According to Form of ye Oath nor Engagement to a Grand
Enquest) wherein they were charged in Bhalfe of or Souer-

aigne Lord the King to Enquire into ye High way's yt were
Stopped & Fenced in but not Námeing ye Town & to make a
returne to yt Court then Mr Attorney Placeing himself at
ye Upper End of ye Table at ye right hand of ye Justices
and Pulled out some papers & Desired ye Justices & Jury
to take Notice of wt he had to Lay before them then caused
an Act of an Assembly to be read by ye Clarke wherein was
granted 5000 Acres of Land to be Laid out in ye Narra-
ganset Country for ye Settling of an Town & This 5000
Acres Should be divided amongst Fifty persons whom
ye Sd Assembly did See cause to accommodate therewth to
be to them & their heirs & Assignes for evr: Provided they
did observe ye Prescriptions & Injunctions yt was laid upon
them by ye Sd Grant & perform ye same accordingly or
othrways to forfiet ye Sd lands Granted then was 1ead an
Ordr for ye Laying out ye Lands and Shewed a paper wch
they called a Platforme of those Lands laid out by themselves wthout form & wthout Scale or Compass or ye Sur-
uayers Name to it or mens to ye divisions Laid out or anything of Sertainty in it for finding out ye highway but according to wt those wch were ye Evidences given into
ye Jury wch they doe Say & Aver to ye wch prsons at
yt time may be Known to be very Young & at yt time not
Capable to Know ye bounds nor Concernes of Each Divisions
as ye lines or bounds then were or where ye highways were
then ye Sd Attorney read an Ordr of their Town where
himself was by them Constituted & Appointed to be their
Attorney & it their behalf to Plead in any of his Majties
Courts of Judicature in defence of their rights & Priviledges
then he read a Coppy of a Letter he had Sent unto ye
Govr declaring their pretended agrieuances as yt there highways was stopped & fenced in by some prsons & desired their
might be a Court of Enquiry & a Jury to find out ye highways & make returne thereof & then he read ye Goverrs

Answer to him y^t it should be done accordingly then he pleaded ye Lands & highways was laid out According to Ord^r & were recorded in their Booke of records & y^t there were Evidences y^t would Shew unto ye Jury where ye highways were but I did not see those Evidences Sworne in ye face of ye Court So ye Jury was sent forth & some of Greenwich men went wth them then ye Court rise Up abruptly & disapated Untill their Dinner was Sett ready for them then ye Jury was sent for to go to Dinner wth them before they had agreed Upon A Verdict Aft^r Dinner some private Consultation wth ye Jury they went out again & staid out till Allmost night only I did obserue y^t two prsons of S^d Jury did come to advise wth ye Justices Privately in ye S^d house & Aft^{r}wards returned to their Fellows & neer night as before S^d came and delivered their verdict wch was as neer as I can remember in these words Following (viz) Wee the Jury Inquiry for o^r Soueraigne Lord ye King doe find y^t Docter Peter Auralt has Presumptiously fenced in ye highway according to Evidences Given to us & therefore Guilty ye wch S^d Verdict ye Court did accept then did I myself make a request unto ye S^d Court to Grant Mee A Coppy of S^d Verdict wch I did in behalf of Doct^r Peter Auralt He being ye Object as I did understand they Pitched upon according to S^d Verdict but could not obtain it Neither was ye S^d Doct^r called for to here ye Play made against him nor ye Evidences given in Unto ye Jury nor their Verdict when Delivered then ye Court rise up again abruptly & went into ye house to Confer about some private Matt^{rs} wch they did Intend to Effect wch I was not aware of Neith^r did I think or Imagine any thing of w^t they Intended wch aft^r my Departure they put in Practice as I am Informed but seeing ye sun was neer Upon Setting & those of my Company being desirous to returne home I went into ye house where ye S^d Justices were & took my Leave of them wch as I do Conjec-

ture they were glad to here of my departure they sent for
Sd Doctr Peter Auralt who Early ye next Morning came to
my house & gave me an accott of their injurious Actions
against him his son & wife wch their may be severll Evidences
yt can testify to ye Truth therefore

Declared and Attested
per John Fones

Newport August:8:1700

Capt John Fones Came before us whose Names are Under
Written and Upon his Corporall Oath did declare that
ye wthin written paper to wch he hath sett his hand unto is
ye truth And nothing but ye truth Taken as Abovesaid

Francis Brinley
Peleg Sanford   } Commissiors
Nathl Coddington

[Indorsed] Capt Fones Euidence about Doctr Perre Ayrault

NOTE ON THE NARRAGANSETT PURCHASES
BY THE
MASSACHUSETTS BAY PROPRIETORS.

THE constant attempt of the authorities of Massachusetts to interfere in the affairs of Rhode Island, and to subjugate the Indians and the chartered territory of the Rhode Island Colony to her jurisdiction, deserve more than a passing notice, as they were the cause not only of the troubles with the French emigrants, but of most of the early troubles and sufferings of our ancestors. We should have had no Indian wars with their attendant massacres, but for their meddling interference.

Their attempts to convert the Indians to Massachusetts Christianity, were not looked upon with favor by the Rhode Island authorities. These attempts were no doubt considered here as a part of a scheme to gain favor with the Indians and establish authority over Narragansett. Roger Williams made many efforts to Christianize the natives, but with little success. In one of his letters dated 1654, he says: " At my last departure for England, I was importuned by the Narragansett Sachems and especially by Ninigret, to present their petition to the High Sachems of England, that they might not be forced from their religion, and for not changing their religion to be invaded by war. For they said they were daily visited by Indians that came from the Massachusetts, that if they would not pray, they should be destroyed by war."[1] Ninigret, on being requested by Mayhew, to give him leave to preach to his people, bade him go and make the English good first. They said it was too difficult for them to understand.[2] The conduct of Christian

1. Potter's Early History Narragansett, 122, 154, 155.
2. Neal's New England, London, 1740, v. 1, p. 275.

nations and people, was then as now, the greatest obstacle to the spread of Christianity.

The ill feeling of the religious people of Massachusetts towards the heretics of Rhode Island, was manifested in various ways. When Rhode Island for her own protection applied to be admitted into the Confederation of the Colonies, she was repulsed. The refusal of the authorities of Massachusetts to sell powder to the people of Rhode Island, is but one example of the prevailing spirit.[1] This may have been done under a pretence of a general law.[2]

They invaded the territory of Rhode Island at pleasure, and made constant attempt to get the Rhode Island Indians to submit to them. The Rhode Islanders and Indians were generally on good terms. The great Indian war of 1676, was considered by the people of Rhode Island, as brought on by the misconduct of the English themselves.[3] The great Sachem Miantonomo had been put to death by the direction of the Massachusetts authorities, and under the advice of the elders of the church.[4] And the editor of Winthrop is obliged to express his condemnation of it. These wars against the Indians were conducted with a savageness not surpassed in more recent times. Their prisoners who were not butchered were sold into slavery to the Bermuda, or West India Islands.[5]

The Puritans of Massachusetts, the term is used to denote

1. Coit's History of Puritanism, pp. 295, 524. Benedict's History of the Baptists, ed. of 1813, v. 1, p. 466. Arnold's History of Rhode Island, v. 1. pp. 158, 258. R. I. Col. Rec , v. 1, p. 324; letter of Roger Williams.

2. Ancient Charters and Laws of Massachusetts Bay, p. 133, dates in margin 1633, 1637.

3. Potter's Early History Narragansett, p. 93; also R. I. Hist. Col., (Callender,) v. 4, p. 126, in note.

4. Winthrop's History of New England, ed. of 1826, v. 2, p. 131.

5. Coit's History of Puritanism, p. 411. Potter's Early Hist. Narragansett, 28, 80, 83, 84, 94.

the dominant clergy who governed the colony without regard to mere minor differences of opinion, have been held up to the world as a set of saints for whom this world was not good enough.   Let us see.

They professed to be driven over here for the sake of religious liberty.   No such thing.   They had that in Holland.   But there they could not lord it over others.   They could not punish heresy in their flock.   And they were afraid of being gradually scattered or swallowed up by their Dutch neighbors.   They came over, as most emigrants go to new countries, to better their condition, and they did it. Never did any set of men know better how to reconcile Godliness and land grabbing than they did.   And as for religious freedom, they never allowed it.   Mrs. Hemans' five verses can be enjoyed by those who can substitute their imagination for facts, but when she says,

> " They left unstained what there they found
>   Freedom to worship God,"

a greater falsehood was never put into poetry, and if we enjoy religious liberty at the present day, we owe no thanks to the Puritans of Massachusetts for it.

For all the outrages and abominations practiced by the Massachusetts government towards the Indians and Rhode Islanders, the Puritan clergy must be held responsible.   The clergy were supreme in the state.   No one but a church member could vote, or be a magistrate or juror.   This of course gave the clergy complete control.[1]   As a matter of course, all the politicians and office holders were very pious and very orthodox.   If General Butler had been a candidate for governor in those days, he would have been obliged to play the role of a saint with cropped hair, white bands and

1. As to the effect of this, see Savage's Winthrop new ed. of 1853, vol. 2, 171, 209.

sanctimonious visage and looked like some of those old ministers whose pictures, for want of something better, used to
be hung up over the doors and in the recesses of the old Har-
vard College library.   And he would have gained in popu-
larity by hanging a few Quakers and witches.   Everything
was done under the advice of the ministers.   When the
great Sachem Miantonomo was treacherously taken prisoner
in a war between him and other Indian tribes, they advised
his death, and are responsible for the savage manner of its
execution, and thus in a great measure for the subsequent
wars and massacres.   When they marched into Rhode Island
to carry out the great Indian butchery of 1676, the first of
their "Laws and ordinances of war," provided that no man
should blaspheme the Trinity, on pain of having his tongue
"bored with a hot iron."

The Puritan clergy thus taking the lead in politics and in
war, the Puritan soldiery butchered the Indians in most approved modern style.   And in treachery they exceeded the
moderns of the West.   One hundred and twenty Indians
surrendered to Captain Eels on a pledge of protection.   The
government, disregarding the pledge, carried them to Plymouth, and sold and transported them all into slavery.   And
the descendants of those men are probably now slaves in the
West India Islands, perhaps in Cuba.[1]   When the Indian
Sachem Canonchet was taken, in order to give the Indian
allies a share in the barbarities, and thus attach them to the
whites, "by the prudent advice of the English command-
ers," the Pequods shot him, Mohicans cut off his head and
quartered him, Ninigret's men burned the quarters, and his
head was sent to the council at Hartford.[2]

---

1. Potter's Early Hist. Narragansett, 80.   Church's Indian War,
Drake's ed., 1829, p. 52.   Morton' Memorial, Davis's ed., 1826, p. 443.
2. Potter's Early Hist. Narragansett, p. 96.   Hubbard's Indian
Wars, 1803, p. 168.   Baylies' Hist. Plymouth, pt. 3, p. 117.

When King Philip was taken, he was quartered,[1] and the pieces hung on four trees. His head and hands were carried first to Rhode Island. The Puritans proclaimed a thanksgiving on the 17th of August, and on that day his head was carried in triumph into Plymouth, and after being exhibited through the country, was exposed on a gibbet where it remained for thirty years.[2] The prayers of Church to save the life of Annawon were disregarded, and he was beheaded. Tispaquin, another chief, surrendered on a pledge of protection from Church,[3] and he was executed with Annawon, "a dastardly act," says Baylies, "which disgraced the government," who thereby basely "violated the English faith."[4] When Philip's son, a boy of nine years of age, was taken prisoner, his case was referred to the clergy for advice. John Cotton and Samuel Arnold were for putting him to death, quoting texts of Scripture to sustain their opinions; others were more merciful; and he was sold as a slave and shipped to Bermuda.[5] In the Pequot war the male Indian children were sold to Bermuda, the women and female children were scattered about among the towns.[6] Some of the Indians who fled for protection to Rhode Island, were sold for nine years; none were sold for life or sent abroad. The Massachusetts authorities complained that the

1. Church's Indian War, Drake's ed., 1829, p. 125.

2. Baylies' Hist. Plymouth, pt. 3, 452. Drake's Ed. of Hubbard, v. I, p. 272.

3. As to Church's authority to promise protection, see Baylies' Hist. Plymouth, pp. 3, 150; also Church's Indian War, Drake's ed., 1829, · p. 96.

4. Baylies' Hist. Plymouth, pt. 3, 183, 184. Church's Indian War, Drake's ed., 1829, p. 144. Morton's Memorial, Davis's ed., pp. 453, 455·

5. Baylies' Hist. Plymouth, pt. 3. 190. Morton's Memorial, Davis's ed., p. 455·

6. Hubbard's Indian Wars, ed. of 1865, v. 2, p. 37. Morton's Memorial, Davis's ed., p. 193. Hutchinson's Hist. Mass., v. 1, ed. of , p. 307.

Rhode Islanders had refused to deliver them up on their demand, that they might "be proceeded against according to the covenant."[1]

Drake's Indian Chronicle consists of reprints of rare tracts and letters written and published during those early times. It is valuable, not so much for its exactness of detail, as for its exposition of the mixture of piety and savageness which actuated the Puritan people; and it gives us some facts additional to those we have.

Captain Mosely took prisoners a father and son. They were examined separately ; the father first. They then examined the son, and lied to him by telling that they had shot his father and threatened that they would shoot him if he did not confess ; and ended by shooting them both.[2] In another case they led an Indian to the gallows, flung the end of the rope over the post and "hoisted him up like a dog three or four times," and finally an Indian stabbed him and sucked his blood.[3]

Eight Indians came to Boston on an embassy with a certificate from Captain Smith.[4] One of them was taken and hanged, because he had killed some one in the war.[5]

In 1637, the Puritan soldiers meeting with seven Pequods, killed five of them, and took one a prisoner alive, him "the English put to the torture, and set all their heads upon the fort."[6] The particulars of this torture are not given. In July, 1676, their Mohegan allies asked the English to give up to them one of the Narragansett captives to be tortured. The English consented. The remainder of the story is too

---

1. R. I. Col. Rec., v. 2, p. 249. Knowles's Life of Roger Williams, p. 347. Potter's Early Hist. Narragansett, pp. 94, 219.
2. Drake's Indian Chronicle, ed., 1836, p. 25 ; ed., 1867, p. 149.
3. Drake's Indian Chronicle, ed. 1836, p. 27 ; ed. 1867, p. 153.
4. Major Richard Smith, well known in Rhode Island history.
5. Drake's Indian Chronicle, ed. 1836, p. 30 ; ed. 1867, p. 157.
6. Winthrop's History of New England, ed. of 1826, v. 1, p. 223.

horrible to be related here, the curious reader is referred to Baylies' History of Plymouth, an excellent authority, pt. 3, p. 136. The dead body of the squaw Sachem Weetomore being found, her head was cut off and carried to Taunton, where it was set upon a pole.[1] "We cannot," says Judge Davis, "peruse without humiliation and disgust the unfeeling sarcasms with which a reverend contemporary historian relates this occurrence."[2]

In the Pequod war, the English attacked and set on fire the Pequod fort, and destroyed about four hundred Indians, killing some, hewing some to pieces, etc. " At this time it was a fearful sight ·to see them thus frying in the fire, and the streams of blood quenching the same. Horrible was the stink and scent thereof; but the victory seemed a sweet sacrifice and they gave the praise thereof to God, who had wrought so wonderfully for them, thus to enclose their enemies in their hands."[3]

When the Indians took female prisoners at Lancaster, and they suffered no wrong, such treatment so surprised the Puritan savages that they were obliged to account for it by a special interposition of God.[4] Baylies in his History of Plymouth, says " all accounts concur in representing the Indians of New England to have invariably respected the honor of women."[5] Whatever of a savage character the

1. Hubbard's Indian Wars, ed. of 1865, v. 1, p. 264.
2. Morton's Memorial, Davis's ed., p. 451.
3. Mortou's Memorial, Davis's ed., p. 189.
4. Hubbard's Indian Wars, ed. 1865, v. 2, p. 260.
5. Baylies' History Plymouth, pt. 3, p. 36. Potter's Early History Narragansett, p. 94. Drake's Indian Chronicle, ed. of 1836, p. 81. Hubbard's Indian Wars, p. 117.

Reference might properly have been made in this connection to the treatment of Mary Dyer, who was banished and finally hanged on accouut of her religious faith, in the estimation of the Massachusetts authorities, the lack of it. The curious scholar is referred to Bishop's New England Judged, for an account of these barbarous acts.

Indians did, was attributed to "the malicious hatred these infidels have to religion and piety."

In 1646, the Council of the United Colonies, Rhode Island not being one, considered the wilful wrongs and hostile practices of the Indians, and their entertaining and protecting offenders, etc., provided that the magistrates of either of the jurisdictions may send "some convenient strength of English," and "seize and bring away any of that plantation of Indians that shall protect," etc., "women and children to be sparingly seized, unless known to be someway guilty, and because it will be chargeable keeping Indians in prison, and if they escaped, they will be more violent and dangerous," satisfaction is to be again demanded of the Sagamore, and if denied, the magistrates are to "deliver up the Indian seized to the party or parties endammaged, either to serve or bee shipped out and exchanged for neagers as the case will justly beare."[1]   Hazard has modernized the spelling into negroes.

The Commissioners of the United Colonies approved and authorized the employment of mastiff dogs against the Indians.[2]

And read the following: "Whereas Mr. Pincheon was questioned about imprisoning an Indian at Agawam, whipping an Indian and freezing of him, the Court is willing to pass over Mr. *Plums*' failings against an Indian." This is a vote of the General Court at Hartford, in 1637.[3]

When we read of such barbarities as we have recited, and then reflect that these were the Indians who protected our ancestors when they were driven away by the bigoted white savages of our neighboring colony, and when we reflect that

1. Hazard's Historical Collections, vol. 2, page 63. Trumbull's Connecticut Records, 1636-65, p. 531. Blue Laws, Andrus's ed., p. 55.
2. Hazard's Historical Collections, vol. 2.
3. Trumbull's Connecticut Records, 1636-65, p. 13.

these wars and brutalities were brought upon them mainly because of this kind treatment of our forefathers, an old-fashioned Rhode Islander may be excused for expressing himself in terms of severity.

And yet within a few years we have had a lecture before our Rhode Island Historical Society, ridiculing these our benefactors, and justifying the Puritans. Canonicus is represented as allowing Williams to "instruct his people in Christian decency and behavior, so long as his supply of groceries lasted." And this was received with apparent gratification and a vote of thanks passed by the Society. How long will it be before they join in the annual grand blarney celebration at Plymouth, and sing hosannas to the Puritans, who whipt, scourged and hung our Quaker and Baptist ancestors.

That the Narragansett Indians were not civilized in the Puritan sense is no doubt true. But they were, compared with the other tribes, an agricultural people. And we have the testimony of Roger Williams to their good and peaceful character, (A. D. 1654): that they were "more friendly in this than our native countrymen. * * Have they not entered leagues of love and to this day continued peaceable commerce with us? Are not our families grown up in peace among them?" "The Narragansetts as they were the first, so they have been long confederates with you; they have been true in all the Pequod wars to you * * * The Narragansetts had never stained "their hands with any English blood, neither in open hostilities nor secret murders. * * * It is true they are barbarians, but their greatest offences against the English have been matters of money or petty revenging of themselves on some Indians on extreme provocations, but God kept them clear of our blood. * * Through all their towns and countries, how frequently do many and oft times one Englishman travel alone with safety and loving kindness.''[1]

"Commonly they never shut their doors day nor night, and 'tis rare that any hurt is done."[2] That they were corrupted afterwards by their intercouse with the whites, and that they were made more savage by the treatment they received, is doubtless true.

Governor Hopkins, in his history of Providence,[3] speaking of the execution of Miantonomo by the advice of the Puritan clergy, says: "This was the reward he received for assisting them some years before in their war with the Pequods. Surely a Rhode Island man may be permitted to mourn his unhappy fate and drop a tear on the ashes of Miantonomo, who, with his uncle Canonicus, were the best friends and greatest benefactors the colony ever had. They kindly received, fed and protected the first settlers of it, when they were in distress and were strangers and exiles, and all mankind else were their enemies, and by this kindness to them, drew down upon themselves the resentment of the neighboring colonies."

The late Chief Justice Staples, one of the most painstaking and accurate of our antiquarians, who resorted to the records for his facts, and not like some modern lecturers to the imagination for them, says of him: "If he had not protected the first settlers of the State of Rhode Island, probably his liberty would not have been deemed inconsistent with the safety of the United Colonies. * * He was sacrificed because he was more liberal in his views than his Christian neighbors, more benevolent in his actions, more catholic in his religion. His memory should be embalmed in the grate-

1. Potter's Early History of Narragansett, pp. 154, 156, 157.
2. Williams's Key to Indian Language, vol. 1, R. I. Hist. Col., p. 50.
3. Massachusetts Historical Collections, second series, vol. 9, p. 202.

ful recollections of every inhabitant of the State of Rhode Island."[1]

And in another work:

"The descendants of the first settlers of Providence, Rhode Island, and Warwick, should ever remember the obligations that their ancestors were under to Miantonomo. * * * When there was no eye to pity and no power to save in the civilized world, Miantonomo was their friend, their protector, their generous benefactor."[2]

Mr. Savage in his notes to Winthrop, [3] says:

"With profound regret I am compelled to express a suspicion that means of sufficient influence could easily have been found for the security of themselves, the pacifying of Uncas and the preservation of Miantonomo, had he not encouraged the sale of Shaomet and Patuxet to Gorton and his heterodox associates."

The names of the Puritan magistrates and clergy who perpetrated these outrages, instead of being damned to everlasting infamy along with the bigots and persecutors of all past ages, are still retained in honor upon the calendar of Massachusetts' saints, and an annual ovation performed in their memory. If the wealthy Quakers and Baptists of the present day had one spark of the spirit of their ancestors, or any regard for their memory, they would place a copy of Coit's Puritanism, Sewel's and Gough's histories of the Quakers, and Benedict's History of the Baptists, in every school and village library throughout the land.

It is common to defend the Puritans by saying that their faults were those of the age in which they lived. If this is a good defence, their defenders should have little to say about Archbishop Laud, or the cruelties of Bloody Queen Mary or any Catholic persecutions.

1. Gorton's Simplicity's Defence.   R. I. Hist. Coll., vol. 2, p. 166.
2. Staples' Annals of Providence, 54.
3. Winthrop's History of New England, ed. of 1853, vol. 2, p. 161.

That the old Puritans (clergy and all) bought and sold slaves may be known to some. But it is not so well known that they were probably the first inventors of a fugitive slave law. In October, 1636, a treaty was made at Boston, with the great Sachem Miantonomo. It contained nine articles. But, as the Indians could not understand them perfectly, a copy of it was sent to Roger Williams, in Rhode Island, to interpret it to them. This was probably a fair specimen of their Indian treaties. It is here referred to for the fifth article, "to return our fugitive servants."[1] In 1643, Massachusetts, Plymouth and the two Connecticut colonies made a confederation for mutual defence ; in 1672, they renewed it. One of the articles provided that "if any servant ran away from his master   *   *   in such case upon the certificate of one magistrate in the jurisdiction out of which the said servant fled, or other due proof, the said servant shall be delivered either to his master or any other that pursues and brings such certificate or proof." But this solemn agreement it seems was hardly needed, for in the letters of a French Protestant Refugee, written in 1687, it is said: "You may also own negroes and negresses. There is not a house in Boston, however small, that has not one or two," some five or six. "Negroes cost from twenty to forty pistoles.   *   *   There is no danger that they will leave you, nor hired help likewise, for the moment one is missing from the town, you have only to notify the savages, who, provided you promise them something, and describe the man to them, he is right soon found."[2]

Selling into slavery was not confined to the Indians or the blacks. In 1659, a son and daughter of Lawrence South-wick were fined for "siding with the Quakers, and absent-

1. Potter's Early Hist. Narragansett, p. 21.
2. Winthrop's Hist. New England. ed. of 1826, vol. 1, 199.

ing themselves from the public ordinances."[1] Not paying their fines the county treasurers were authorized to sell them into Virginia or Bermuda.

That the negroes were generally humanely treated is very probable, but they had little protection from the laws. Dr. Belknap[2] in 1795, says "the negro children were considered incumbrances, and were given away like puppies," and that the severest and most effective threat to a negro, was that he should be sold to the West Indies or Carolina.

In the "Body of Liberties" of Massachusetts, A. D. 1641, we find it enacted: "There shall never be any bond slavery, villanage nor captivity among us, unless it be lawful captives taken in just wars and such strangers as willingly sell themselves or are sold unto us ; and these shall have all the liberties and Christian usages which the law of God established in Israel requires." This legal recognition of slavery is said to be several years earlier than can be found in the laws of Virginia or Maryland.[3] Of the existence of slavery in Rhode Island, I have written in another place.[4] The Rhode Islanders apprenticed or sold some of the Indians for a term of years in the great Indian war of 1675–6. They sold none absolutely. They did in May, 1659, pass a law authorizing the sale of an Indian guilty of grand larceny, but it was only after conviction and it was the guilty person who was to be sold. Even this is not to be justified, but it is not quite as bad as when one Indian committed a theft, to catch and sell another one [5]

In an act of the Massachusetts Legislature passed in

1. Sewel's History of the Quakers, vol. 1. p. 278. Hinman's Blue laws, p. '7.

2. Massachusetts Hist. Coll., 1st series, vol. 4, p. 200.

3. Hildreth's History of United States, vol. 1, p. 678.

4. Lecture before the R. I. Hist. Society by the author, February 19, 1851.

5. Rhode Island Colonial Records, vol. 1, p. 412.

May, 1705, entitled "an act for the better preventing of a spurious and mixed issue," etc., it was enacted that if any negro or mulatto struck a person of the English or other Christian nation he should be severely whipped. To further illustrate the spirit of the people, the two following extracts from private letters are introduced, the first, from Hugh Peters, was written to John Winthrop, from Salem, probably about 1645. He says:

"Mr. Endecot and my selfe salute you in the Lord Jesus. Wee have heard of a dividence of women and children in the bay and would be glad of a share, viz.: a young woman or girle and a boy if you thinke good. I wrote to you for some boyes for Bermudas which I think is considerable."[1]

The second is from Emanuel Downing, son-in-law of Governor Winthrop. It was written in 1637-8. He says: "A warr with the Narragansett is verie considerable to this plantation, for I doubt whither yt be not synne in vs, hauing power in our hands, to suffer them to maynteyne the worship of the devill, which their paw wawes often doe; 2lie, If upon a Just ware the Lord should deliver them into our hands, we might easily haue men, woemen and children enough to exchange for Moores, which will be more gayneful pilladge for us than wee conceive, for I do not see how wee can thrive untill wee gett into a stock of slaues sufficient to do all our business for our children's children will hardly see this great Continent filled with people, soe that our servants will still desire freedom to plant for themselves, and not stay but for verie great wages. And I suppose you know verie well how we shall maynteyne 20 Moores (negroes) cheaper than one Englishe servant.

"The ships that shall bring Moores may come home laden

---

1. Massachusetts Historical Collections, series 4, vol. 6, p. 95.

with salt which may beare most of the chardge, if not all of yt. But I marvayle Conecticott should anywayes hasard a warre without your helps."[1]

We have seen that while the hatred of heresy was one source of hostility towards Rhode Island, the passion for land speculation was another. Roger Williams[2] says: "You will find the business at bottom to be * * a depraved appetite after * * great portions of land in this wilderness. * * * This is one of the Gods of New England." Deeds of immense tracts were obtained from the Indians by Massachusetts men on the one hand, and Rhode Island men on the other. Sometimes there was a consideration, sometimes none, and how much the Indians understood of the nature of a deed may easily be guessed. For the manner in which treaties were forced upon them, and how little they understood of them, repeated illustrations can be seen in the histories of the times.[3]

The Colonial Magistrates sent for the Indian Sachems at pleasure, made charges against them and compelled them to sign writings of the effect of which they knew nothing. So King Philip was compelled to sign a writing acknowledging himself a subject of the English. When at Boston, in 1671, he was told that he had done so, he indignantly denied it, [4] said that it was merely an agreement of friendship and amity.

Baylies, in his History of Plymouth, gives a character of Philip very different from that generally given by the clerical historians.[5]

The Rev. Samuel Peters has been very much censured for his history of the first colonists of Connecticut. That he ex-

1. Massachusetts Hist. Coll., series 4, vol. 6, p. 65.
2. Potter's Early Hist. Narragansett, p. 162.
3. Potter's Early History of Narragansett, pp. 21, 47, 49, 79.
4. Hutchinson, 1, 281. Baylies' Plymouth, pt. 3, p. 53.
5. Baylies' Plymouth, pt. 3, p. 169.

aggerated the faults and foibles of those whom he considered his persecutors, is very probable. He is commonly understood as representing that they met in solemn meeting and voted unanimously—

    1st.   That the earth is the Lord's and the fullness thereof.

    2d.   That he has given it to his saints ; and

    3d.   That we are the saints,

and accordingly they took possession.

This is rather an exaggeration of what Peters does say, but not much.[1] He says that when the Sachems refused to give the land to them, they voted themselves to be the children of God, and that the wilderness in the uttermost parts of the earth was given to them. Be this as it may, nothing better represents the ruling spirit of the Puritans in their treatment of the Indians. It represents what was in the minds of all the people. It is true as a myth, in the sense of the myths of ancient history. The same thing is now going on at the West ; except that it is not the fashion of the present day to profess any peculiar sanctity. They ask no leave of God or any body else.

Another charge against Peters is, that he represents the first settlers as meeting and voting that they would be governed by the Laws of God, until they had time to make better ones. What he does say (page 54) is that the Colony "adopted the Bible for its code of civil laws, till others should be made more suitable for their circumstances." This was probably founded on some expression in the first Code of Connecticut, where it appears that they provided for being governed by the rule of the Word of God in cases for which they had not provided in their code;[2] or, as Secretary Hinman states it, "for want of a law in any particular case, shall be judged by the Word of God."[1]

1. Peters' History Connecticut, New Haven, 1829, pp. 46, 66.

2. Hinman's Blue Laws, pp. 130, 150; also Baylies' History Plymouth, pt. 2 p. 74. Laws of Plymouth.

The Rhode Island code of laws of 1647, is a most excellent one. It contains plentiful references to the laws of England,[1] but no reference whatever to the Laws of God. But then its authors were heretics.

The Puritans perhaps were not the first to bribe members of the cabinet and government officers. They were very cautious and perhaps conscientious as to using such a wicked word. But Puritan shrewdness was equal to the occasion. Chalmers openly charges them with attempting to bribe the officers and influential men of the English government.[2] The Massachusetts Council, December 31, 1663, appointed a committee "to *improve* some friend or friends in England,"[3] to obtain information "and *prevent all inconvenience* the best they may." The General Court, May 18, 1664, referring to this, authorized the committee to engage some faithful friends in England, at an expense not exceeding £400. The General Court had before this in 1661, authorized a committee for managing their affairs at London, to *remove all obstacles* or objections that might lie in their way, and their proceedings were to be kept secret unless the General Court should call for them.[4] In 1682,[5] they had authorized the committee managing their English affairs " to *improve* any *meet instrument* for the obtaining " a general pardon and continuance of their charter.

Hereafter Railroad companies will not wickedly attempt to bribe members of Congress, they need only *improve* them.

Their agents in England, either forged or surreptitiously procured before it had passed the proper ordeal, a pretended

1. Proceedings of First General Assembly of Rhode Island in 1647, ed. of Judge Staples. Providence, 1847.

2. Chalmers' Political Annals, pp. 412, 413, 461; also History of Revolution of Colonies, vol. 1, p. 132.

3. Massachusetts Colonial Records, vol. 4, pt. 2, p. 101.

4. Massachusetts Colonial Records, v. 4, pt. 2, p. 39.

5. Chalmers' Political Annals, p. 461.

patent bearing date in 1643,[1] giving to Massachusetts the government of the Narragansett country, including of course the site of our Frenchtown settlement. Of this pretended patent Roger Williams says:[2] "The Lord High Admiral President said openly in a full meeting of the Commissioners, that he knew no other charter for these parts than what Mr. Williams had obtained, for he was sure that charter which the Massachusetts Englishmen pretended, had never passed the table." For other reasons and authorities, see Mr. Aspinwall's pamphlet[3] upon this subject. No one pretends that the government of Massachusetts would procure or countenance a forgery. It was a clique of unprincipled land speculators acting under the cloak of their name and under the garb of piety and hatred of heresy. And this was the sort of people who caused a very large part of the conflicts and civil disturbances which hindered and delayed the peaceable settlement of Narragansett, and of which Rhode Island has had most unjustly to bear the blame.

The feeling produced by these arrogant assumptions, by these scourgings, banishings, hangings of our heretical ancestors has not yet entirely disappeared among the older portion of our country people. And it ought not to, so long as the authors of these barbarities are defended and canonized as they are. I have in my youth seen elderly people who could not speak of the "Massachusetts Presbyterians," as they called them without a gritting of teeth.

We have had a few among our people who have taken some pains to justify the memory of our ancestors. The

---

1. Miscellaneous State Papers, v. 1. Secretary of State of Massachusetts.

2. Letter to Mason. Potter's Early History Narragansett, pp 37, 161. See also the documents in Staples' ed. of Gorton's Simplicity's Defence, p. 305, 195.

3. This exhaustive argument was republished by Sidney S. Rider, Providence, 1865. A few copies yet remain unsold.

late Hon. Henry Bull of Newport, was one of the first, and latterly, Benedict in his History of the Baptists, the late Judge Staples, Governor Arnold in History of Rhode Island, Zachariah Allen, Esq., and Professor Diman, have done good service in bringing to light the truth on these subjects.

The conduct of the Puritans and the savage character of their treatment of the Indians, will by many be justified on the theory that they could not be dealt with in any other manner.   Whether this excuse is available for a people pretending to Christianity is doubtful.   That after the Great Swamp fight both parties acted like savages, is undeniable. The Indians had been nearly destroyed in the fight, their huts with their women and children, and their stores of provisions burnt up, and the survivors driven out in the cold of mid-winter to freeze and starve.

On the part of the whites the fury extended even to the women.   The women of Marblehead, coming out of church, fell on two Eastern Indians who had been brought in as captives and "very barbarously" murdered them [1] And very lately a monument has been erected (as the newspapers say) to a woman who tomahawked and scalped ten sleeping Indians and then escaped.   The wars with the Eastern Indians were going on at the time of Philip's war.

It is becoming the fashion to erect monuments to the dead Indians, now that they are out of the way and can give us no trouble.   Matthew xxiii., 30; Luke ix., 59: 60.

1. This occurred in 1677. See Hutchinson's Massachusetts Bay, vol. 1, p. 307.

GENEALOGICAL NOTES.

When, many years ago, the writer was collecting materials for the "Early History of Narragansett" published in 1835, it was with the utmost difficulty that the materials could be obtained for the few pages of family history contained in that work. Few families had preserved any family records, and few seemed to care about them. And most of the information in that work was obtained from the records with a good deal of labor. From one person, the late Thomas B. Hazard, of Peace Dale, who died A. D. 1845, at the age of 90, he obtained a great deal of traditional information about Mr. Hazard's own, and other families, which in every instance he found to be confirmed by the records, when searched.

Since then the feeling has changed ; every family has some one engaged in hunting up its history, and the passion has been carried to a ridiculous extreme. Those who get up the present fashionable genealogies begin way back in English history with an account of all the princes, lords and knights who have borne the name or any name similar to it. We expect, of course, to find the descendants of some of these nobles coming over about 1620, and settling in this country. But here comes a sudden break ; and the family history begins again generally somewhat in this style : The first of the name we find in this country was ———. A few years ago some one published a genealogical table of one of our old families, and represented his ancestor as owning almost the whole country. Such things as these may flatter vanity, but they subject the writers, justly, and sometimes a whole family unjustly to censure.

Savage, in his Genealogical Dictionary, volume 4, page 144, well says : "Much benefit to thousands of enquirers on our side of the ocean may be derived from the wise use of a few words in the note of Mr. Hunter, on pages 6 and 7 of 'The Founders of New Plymouth,' edition 1854: 'Mere possession of a surname which coincides with that of an English family, is no proof of connection with that family. Claims of alliance founded on this basis are not the legitimate offspring of laborious genealogical enquiry, but of self love and the desire to found a reputation for ancestorial honor, where no such honor is really due.' Well is the topic explained in further remarks, founded on experience of more than one gross case of indecent pretension."

It was formerly very common for sea captains and travellers to go to the Herald's office, in London, and procure coats of arms of some one of their name. These were brought home and sometimes framed and conspicuously displayed, and may hereafter perhaps be used as evidence of connection with the English family. They are of course worth but little.

There are but two families in this part of the country, who to the knowledge of the writer, can trace their families into Europe for many generations before the emigration. The family of Dr. John Clarke, the colonial agent, can, upon undoubted evidence, go back several generations in England. Its representatives are still numerous in South Kingstown and Westerly; and the Bernons were of an ancient and honorable family in Rochelle, in France.

One great difficulty in tracing by our records, arises from having sometimes many of the same Christian name living at the same time. In the Reynolds, Gardner, Hazard and Babcock families, this is especially the case. In such cases the tracing of the title to some tract of land, may aid materially. A very complete genealogy of the Brenton family can be made from the Land Records of South Kingstown.

Another difficulty arises from the various removals of

families from one town to another.   In this respect the
Quaker Records afford great aid as to the members of that
Society.   The general course of emigration was through
Massachusetts to Portsmouth and Newport, and from thence
across to the west side of the Bay.   The Misquamicott settlement originated in Newport.   The settlers had to pass a
wilderness, and the name they gave it, Westerly, is signifi-
cant of the state of the country at the time.

After the close of our Revolutionary war, and in fact ever
since, there has been a very large emigration from the Narragansett country to the Western States.   The greatest number of the early emigrants went to Vermont, to the borders
of Hoosic River in New York, to the Genesee country, in
which name was then included all the country around the
small lakes in western New York, to Wyoming and Wilkes-
barre, and the borders of the Susquehannah River, and to
Marietta in Ohio.   And from thence their descendants have
become scattered all over the Western States.   There was
also quite a large settlement of French from Rhode Island
near Chatham Four Corners and Hudson, in New York.

THE MAWNEY FAMILY.

LE MOINE.   The christian name of the first Le Moine is not given on the plat, but by the tradition in the family, it was Moses.   The French settlers, according to the family tradition, settled around a spring on the present Mawney farm, and planted an orchard there, always since known as the French orchard, and, within the remembrance of the writer, there were trees there supposed to be remains of the original orchard.   When the settlement was broken up, the Mawneys must have remained there; as the name of Peter Money is on the oldest plat of East Greenwich known to be in existence, and attached to the tract of land which has been in the family ever since.   The name seems to have been first changed to Money, and later to Mawney.   The same tradition preserves the names of two children of. Moses: First, Peter; and second, Mary, who married an Appleby, of New York.

Col. Peter Mawney, lived the greater part of his life in East Greenwich, but removed to Providence before his death, and his will is recorded there.   He died in Providence, September 9, 1754, aged 65, and is buried, with other relatives, in the old North Burial Ground.   This would make his birth about 1689.

He was twice married, first to Mary Tillinghast, who died February 24, 1726-7, in the 34th year of her age, and is buried in the Tillinghast burial ground, next north of the Mawney farm; second, to Mercy, daughter of Pardon Tillinghast, who survived him, and died in 1761, the widow of James Brown, and is buried in the North Burial Ground.

The children of Col. Peter Mawney were:

1.   Elizabeth, born November 22, 1714, wife of Josep, Olney.

2.   Mercy, married Thomas Fry, Jr., December 23h 1742.   In Col. Mawney's will he mentions his granddaughter, Mercy Fry.

3.   Lydia, married Dr. Ephraim Bowen, June 10, 1746. See Bowen, post.

4.   Mary, married James Angell, October 5, 1752, grandmother of the late Prof. William G. Goddard.[1]

5.   John, born August 11, 1718; died June 13, 1754. See below.

6.   Pardon, born October 5, 1753; went to sea and never heard from.

7.   Sarah, married Joseph Whipple.   Their son Samuel was father of the late Hon. John Whipple, Brown University, 1802, and their son George was grandfather of Joseph W. Congdon, attorney at law at East Greenwich.

8.   Amey, married Dr. Samuel Carrew, April 22, 1760; died 1762, aged 26; buried in North Burial Ground,

John Mawney, son of Col. Peter, died before his father, and his will is recorded in Providence.   He married, October 29, 1745, Amey, daughter of Robert Gibbs, who is described on his tombstone in the North Burial Ground, as de scended from the family of Sir Henry Gibbs, of Dorsetshire, England, Amey, wife of Robert Gibbs, was daughther of Col. Joseph Whipple, and widow of ——— Crawford.   The children of John and Amey Mawney were:

1.   Pardon, born at Providence, December 27, 1748; died on the homestead, in East Greenwich, given him by his grandfather's will, August 6, 1831.   He married Experience, daughter of Caleb Gardner, of South Kingstown.   See below.

2.   Dr. John Mawney, a physician, sometime sheriff of Providence county, and was in the expedition that burnt the Gaspee.   He died in Cranston, in March 1830, in his 80th

1.   Updike's Narragansett Church, p. 155.

year, and was buried in the North Burial Ground. He
married, first, Nancy Wilson; second, Elizabeth Clarke.
Children:

a.   John, married Ruth, daughter of John Gladding, and
left one child, Elizabeth, who married William A. Cole, and
now resides in Shakapee, Minnesota.

b.   Mary, daughter of John and Elizabeth, married
Henry Valentine, A. D. 1807. Their children were, first,
Maria A.; second, Edward H.; third, John M.; fourth,
Elizabeth; fifth, Horatio; sixth, Harriet A.; seventh, Alfred
A., now in New York city. Mrs. Mary Valentine died in
Brooklyn, N. Y., 1864. Henry Valentine died in 1847.

c.   Susan, born January 5, 1788; married Benjamin P.
Ware, 1812. He died in 1816. She died October, 1869.
Of the children, Albert P. Ware, born August 3, 1813, is
now living in Andover, Massachusetts, and Charles M. Ware,
born August 23, 1815, is living at Norwich, Connecticut.

3.   Hannah, daughter of John Mawney, married Stephen
Harris, January 23, 1775. She died at the age of 34,
leaving one son, Stephen, father of the late Almoran Harris.

4.   Mary died December 25, 1757, aged eleven years.

5.   Nancy died, aged seventeen years.

Pardon, before referred to, died at East Greenwich, August 6, 1831. His wife, Experience, was born November
1, 1751; married June, 1772. She died November 28,
1815. Their children were:

1.   Peter Lemoine, born April 16, 1778; died in Moreau,
Saratoga county, New York, January 30, 1868. Children:
First, John G., died at Tyrone, Steuben country, 1837;
second, Pardon, deceased ; third, Horatio, (Geneva, N. Y.);
fourth, Isabella Ann ; fifth, Sarah ; sixth, Peter, deceased.
John G. left children: First, Dr. John G., Mazomanie,
Dane county, Wisconsin; second, Caleb; third, William W.,

Dundee, Yates county, N. Y.; fourth, Zeruah; fifth, Mary; sixth, Sarah; seventh, Robert.

2. John G., born October 1, 1774, was for many years clerk of one of the courts of Kent county. He died December 28, 1846. Children: First, Mary; second, William; third, Tabitha; fourth, Benjamin; fifth, Robert G.; sixth, Julia married Ebenezer Hopkins; seventh, John G.; eighth, Harriet, married Oliver A. Weeks, died October, 1875.

3. One unnamed.

4 and 5. Amey and Nancy born March 23, 1777. Nancy died 1787. Amey married first, Capt. William E. Tillinghast, of Providence. He died 1817. Second, Elisha Atkins, of Providence, and afterwards of Newport, B. U. 1816. No children. She died October 3, 1864.

6. Mary, born April 24, 1779; married, July 9, 1810, Elisha R. Potter, of South Kingstown, member of Congress, 1796-1797 and 1809-1815. She died July 26, 1835. He died September 26, 1835. Children: First, Elisha R., H. C. 1830, second, Thomas; third, Dr. Thomas M., B. U., 1834, U. S. Navy; fourth, William Henry, B. U. 1836, attorney at law; fifth, James B. Mason, B. U. 1839; sixth, Mary Elizabeth.

7. Moses, born November 4, 1780; married Elizabeth Arnold, November 1816; died August 1, 1821. Children: First, Robert G.; second, Hannah, married Joseph R. Arnold; third, Elizabeth Ann.

8. Hannah, born April 13, 1782; married first, Nicholas Tillinghast. One son, Edward N., born September 11, 1805. Married, second, Jeffrey Davis, December, 1824. She died Sept. 20, 1860.

9. Elizabeth Cranston, born July 7, 1784; married October 19, 1805, Jeffrey Davis, of North Kingstown. She died July 1814. Children: First, Abby, married Thomas

B. Wilbor, of Coventry; second, George Albert; third, William Dean, who married Mary E. Congdon.

10. Nicholas G., born March 18, 1786; died August 27, 1874, on the homestead; unmarried; will recorded at East Greenwich.

11. Robert Gibbs, born 1788; went to sea in 1811 and never heard from.

12. Caleb, born 1789, died 1790.

13. Tabitha, born 1791; died 1808.

14. Samuel Ayrault, born May 8, 1792; married, in 1816, Phebe Nichols; died January 8, 1866. Children: First, Elizabeth, married Edward Wheeler, Auburn, New York; second, Maria, married Maynard Chappell, Henrietta, New York; third, Isabella Ann, married James G. Maynard, Providence, Bureau county, Illinois.

15. Isabella A., born November 30, 1797; married Peter G. Taylor, June 27, 1822; he died at Brooklyn, New York, December 20, 1871; she died July 29, 1873. Children: First, Pardon L., born 1824, died November, 1860, at Brooklyn, New York; second, Isabella Ann, born 1826, married, 1848, George W. Frost, of New Market, New Hampshire; third, Amey Elizabeth, born 1831, married Walter J. Gilbert.

The account of the French settlers here given, the locality of the settlement and the name of the first emigrant of the Mawney family, together with the early history of the family, were taken down by an uncle of the writer from the lips of Pardon Mawney a few years before the death of the latter, in 1831; and when it is considered that Pardon Mawney was born in 1748, and was soon old enough to have conversed with some of the emigrants themselves, and with their families, the tradition becomes more than ordinarily reliable. Pardon Mawney's grandfather, who died after the birth of Pardon, must have been born in 1689, about the

time of the settlement.   And until within comparatively a
few years there has been very little change in the families
which have owned the land and lived in the neighborhood.

Pardon Mawney was for many years in his youth in the
house of his uncle Gibbs, in Boston, and while there attended school.   It was during his residence there that Gov.
Hutchinson's house was sacked by the mob, in August, 1765;
and he was present when the furniture was thrown from the
windows, and picked up among the rubbish a pack of play-
ing cards representing scenes in the famous Rye House Plot,
which are still preserved.

Dr. Ephraim Bowen, son of Thomas, died 1812, age 96 years. Married, first, Mary, daughter of Thomas Fenner, February 9, 1737–8. Second, Lydia, daughter of Col. Peter Money, June 10, 1746. Children by first wife:

1. Gov. Jabez, born November 17, 1739; died in 1815; married, December 19, 1762, Sarah, daughter of Obadiah Brown. She died March 17, 1800.

Children: *a.* Obadiah, born 1763; died 1793. *b.* Oliver, born 1767. *c.* Mary, born 1772. *d.* Jabez, born 1774. *e.* Henry, born 1776; died 1777. *f.* Horatio G., born 1779; Librarian of Brown University; died March 23, 1848. *g.* Another, born 1782. *h.* Henry, 2nd, born 1785; for thirty years Secretary of State of Rhode Island.

He married, second, Peddy Leonard, May 21, 1801.

2. Oliver, born November 17, 1742. His son, Oliver, Jr., was father of Mary Demont Bowen, lately deceased.

Children by second wife:

3. Dr. William, born March 8, 1747, married Susan Corlis, 1769, died 1832, aged 86 years. Children: *a.* Elizabeth, married Thomas Amory, 1799, whose children were: Mary; Harriet, married Robert H. Ives; John, Julia, married Rt. Rev. M. A. D'W. Howe; Louise; Anna; Helen, married William Raymond Lee; Thomas. *b.* Sarah, married William S. Skinner, 1816. *c.* Maria, married Hon. John Whipple, B. U., 1802, whose children were: John; Maria, married Rev. Francis Vinton; Elizabeth, married Prof. William Gammell; Sarah C., married, first, Robert P. Swann, of Virginia; second, William H. Potter; Samuel, died young; Harriet, married William S. Slater; William. *d.* Harriet, married, 1815, Commodore Charles Morris, United States Navy, whose children were: Charles; Har-

riet, married Rev. Dr. Coolidge; Louise, married William W. Corcoran, of Washington; Elizabeth, married Dr. John L. Fox; Helen; R. Murray; Dr. William B.; Maria, married Rev. Mr. Duncan; George; Julia, married Dr. Addison. *e.* Dr. William C. Bowen, born June 2, 1785; died 1815; married Rebecca Olney, 1812; had a son William.

4.   Mary, born 1748; unmarried.

5.   Sarah, born 1750; married Thomas Lloyd Halsey.

6.   Lydia, born 1752; married John Innes Clarke, 1773, of whose daughters, Harriet married, 1811, Dr. Robert Hare, of Philadelphia, and Anna E., married, 1803, Oliver Kane.

7.   Col. Ephraim, born 1753; married, first, Sally Angell; was in the Revolutionary army, and one of the captors of the Gaspee.   Children :   First, William B., born in 1777, died August 26, 1826.   Second, Julia, born in 1779; married John D. Martin, 1803.   Third, Nathaniel, died young.   Fourth, Sally A., died young.   Fifth, Elizabeth, born in 1787; married Hon. John H. Clarke, B. U. 1809, afterwards Senator in Congress.   Mr. Clarke died in 1872.   Their son, Hon. James M. Clarke, B. U. 1838, was for several years U. S. District Attorney in Rhode Island.

Col. Bowen married, second, Sarah Whipple in 1794. Children: First, Esther; second, George T.; third, Sarah ; fourth, Mary.

Col. Bowen died September 2, 1841, at his home at Pawtuxet, in Warwick.

8.   Benjamin, born 1755.

9.   Dr. Pardon, born March 26, 1757; died October, 1826, aged 69 years; married Elizabeth Ward, 1780.   Had two sons, William, who went South, and Henry, who died young; and three daughters, Esther, married Charles W. Greene, 1806; Frances, who married Charles W. Greene,

1813, and Anna E., who married Franklin Greene, and is still living at East Greenwich.

10. Benjamin, born 1759; went to New York.

11. Ann, born 1762; married Edward Mitchell, 1792. Mrs. Mitchell died in Charleston, S. C., in 1855.

12. Betsey, born 1765; married John Ward, 1792; no children.

13. Fanny, 1768; married John E. Moore, 1789.

Dr. William Bowen, Dr. Pardon Bowen, and Dr. William C. Bowen, were all of great eminence in their profession. See Thatcher's New England Medical Biography and Dr. Usher Parsons' Sketches of Rhode Island Physicians.

THE AYRAULT FAMILY.

In Mrs. Lee's Huguenots in France and in America,[1] Dr. Pierre Ayrault is spoken of as a native of Angers, in France. He will be at once recognized as the author of the memorial relating to the breaking up of the French settlement. Like the Mawneys and other families, he remained and continued on good terms with the neighboring Rhode Island settlers, thus showing that the disturbance could have grown out of no national antipathy. He probably soon removed to the neighboring village of East Greenwich, as more convenient for his professional practice. And in 1699[2] we find him joining with others in the foundation of Trinity Church, in Newport, where the petitioners are spoken of as "within this island." This, however, is not conclusive. In 1704 Madamé Knight, in her journeyings south from East Greenwich, on towards New York, speaks of being joined by the French doctor. In 1711-12 we find from the records at East Greenwich, that Daniel Ayrault sold to David Greene his house and nineteen acres of land. This probably was the time of the final removal of the family to Newport.

Peter Ayrault's will, made in 1705, proved June 4, 1711, and recorded in the old parchment book at East Greenwich, mentions his wife Frances, and his son Samuel, mariner now abroad, giving to the latter a legacy, and giving the remainder of his property to his son Daniel, merchant.

Daniel, the only son of Pierre of whom we have any mention, was born about 1676-7 and settled in Newport. In the old parchment book of records at Greenwich, we find that Daniel Ayrault, with a number of others, received let-

1. Mrs. Lee's Huguenots, volume 2, page 108.
2. Arnold's History of Rhode Island, vol. 1, p. 559.

ters of denization July 3, in the thirteenth year of William
Third, A. D., 1702. He married, May 9, 1703, Mary,
daughter of ———————— and Judith Robineau, and granddaughter of Elias and Susanna Neau, of New York. Their
marriage contract, dated April, 1703, is given at length in
Mrs. Lee's Huguenot's in France and America.[1] Daniel
died June 25, 1764, aged 87 years, 9 months and 17 days.
She died January 5, 1729, aged 44 years. He married,
second, Rebecca, widow of Edward Neargrass, in 1745.
The children of Daniel and Mary were :

1.   Mary, born at East Greenwich, February 16, 1704 ;
married James Cranston, 1720-1 ; children, Walter and
Mary ; married, second, George Goulding, whom she survived, and died in 1764.

2.   Pierre, born at East Greenwich, October 4, 1705.

3.   Daniel, born at East Greenwich, November 2, 1707 ;
married, first, Susanna, Neargrass, in 1735 ; second, Rebecca Neargrass, in 1737 ; third, Hart, daughter of Jahleel
and Frances Brenton, in 1745 ; she died in 1764. He died
in 1770. Children : a. Stephen. b. Daniel, died young.
c. Mary, died 1792. Children by Hart Brenton : a. Peter ;
b. Hart; c. Rebecca ; d. Martha, born in 1759, died same
year, and three others who died young. Peter and Hart
both died unmarried.

4.   Stephen, born at East Greenwich, December 11,
1709. The births of numbers two, three and four, are on
record at East Greenwich.

5.   Anthony, born in 1712 ; died in 1726.

6.   Elias, born at Newport, February 13, 1713-14 ; went
to sea.

7.   Judith, born at Newport, in 1716 ; died young.

8.   Frances, born at Newport, September 2, 1718 ; mar-

1.   Mrs. Lee's Huguenots, volume 2, page 107.

ried Walter Cranston, March 26, 1747.   She died February 2, 1798.

9.   Samuel, born in Newport, March 22, 1720 ; died August 11, 1798, and buried at the Tillinghast burying ground, on the farm north of the Mawney farm, in East Greenwich.   He is described on his tombstone as a merchant.

10.   Anthony, died when 4 years old.

11.   Susanna, born June 29, 1723 ; died May 3, 1809.

12.   Judith, born December 9, 1725 ; died November 26, 1806 ; married Joseph Tillinghast.

Children of Stephen, fourth child of Daniel and Mary. His tombstone gives his age 84.   The Mercury of April 22, 1794, contains a notice of him.   He married December 23, 1740, Ann, eldest daughter of Peter Bours.   She was born April 2, 1724, and died December 17, 1754.

Children : *a.* Frances, baptized 1747 ; married, first, in 1767, Edward, son of Gov. Gideon Wanton ; second, John Piper.   *b.* Ann.   *c.* Mary, baptized in 1742 ; married, in 1764, George Scott.   Mary had one daughter, Ann, who married, first, William Robinson ; second, Dr. John P. Mann.   She died in 1841.   *d.* Bathsheba, died young.

The children of Edward Wanton and Frances, his wife, were : First, Stephen A. ; second, Sarah ; third, Frances, married William C. Robinson.   Their children were : *a.* Edward W., born in 1797, died in 1818.   *b.* Stephen A., born in 1799 ; married Sarah, daughter of Jeremiah N. Potter, 1822 ; was Grand Master of Masons, and died April 7, 1877, in South Kingstown.   No children.   *c.* Frances W., died young.   *d.* George C., died in 1820.   *e.* William C. Robinson, born in 1803 ; married Abby B., daughter of Josiah C. Shaw.   He died in 1871.

Mary, daughter of Daniel, 2nd, died 1792.   She married Benjamin Mason, 1754.   Children: Benjamin, Daniel,

Susan and Mary.   Benjamin, last named, married Margaret Champlin.   Their son, George Champlin Mason, was father of George C. Mason, Esq., now living in Newport.

In Hinman's Records of Wethersfield, Conn., and also in the New England Genealogical Register, volume xv., are mentioned several of this name. From the similarity of Christian names, they were probably relatives of the Rhode Island family.

THE BERNON FAMILY.

The person who, from his standing in his native country and his wealth was probably the most conspicuous among the French settlers in Massachusetts and Rhode Island, was Gabriel Bernon. He was born April 6, 1644, of an ancient family at Rochelle, of which city it is traditionary in one branch of the family here, he was hereditary registrar. In anticipation of the troubles he fled to London.[1] He landed in Boston in 1688. He was one of the principal persons concerned in the French settlement at Oxford, Massachusetts, for which we must refer to the very full account in Massachusetts Historical Collections.[1] Quite full accounts of him and much of his correspondence are published in the work last referred to, and also in Updike's History of the Narragansett Church, and in Mrs. Lee's Huguenots in France and America.

In the very full genealogy of the Bernon family, published in France, the posterity of Gabriel Bernon are not given. But his correspondence with his brother Samuel; with Benjamin Faneuil, (of Faneuil Hall memory,) who married his sister Marie; and with another brother-in-law, Pierre Sanceau, all of whom are mentioned in the printed genealogy, and which correspondence is now in the possession of his descendants, all prove the connection. The genealogy extends back to 1545. The Faneuils after coming to this country returned and lived in France.

Bernon and Faneuil and Louis Allaire were concerned together in various mercantile operations. He remained in Boston about ten years and removed to Newport about 1697. He was one of the first petitioners for the establishment of

1. Massachusetts Historical Collections, vol. 22, p. 69.

an Episcopal church in Newport, September, 1699,[1] and from this and other similar movements originated the English society for the propagation of the Gospel in foreign parts in 1702. Bernon's first wife, Esther Le Roy, died in Newport, June 14, 1710, aged fifty six years, and her gravestone is still to be seen there. For a short time after the death of his wife he resided in Providence, and then began to make purchases with a view to trade in Kingstown. In those days the great road for travel from Boston to New York followed the shore, and was sometimes known as the Pequot path. Wickford, or as then sometimes called, Updike's Newtown, and Tower Hill, were two of the principal places of business on it. He purchased of Lodowick Updike a wharf lot at Wickford, built a wharf, a warehouse, and a sloop.[2] While in Kingstown he was active in support of St. Paul's Episcopal church, of which Rev. James McSparran was rector; but about 1719 we find him again settled in Providence, where he remained until his death.

In 1712 he married for his second wife Mary Harris, daughter of Thomas Harris, 2nd, and grand niece of William Harris, the companion of Roger Williams.

Of the children of Bernon's first marriage, Jane married, October 11, 1722, Col. William Coddington, of Newport.

Esther married, May 30, 1713, Adam Ap Howell, or Powell.[3] Their daughter Elizabeth, born in Newport, April 8, 1714, married Rev. Mr. Seabury, of New London, whose son Samuel by a former marriage was the first English bishop in America.[4] Esther, (daughter of Adam and Esther Powell,) was born in Newport, May, 1718.[5]

1. Arnold's History of R. I., vol. 1, p. 559: vol. 2, pp. 76, 116.
2. Updike's History of the Narragansett Church, p. 42.
3. Trinity Church Records, Newport.
4. Updike's History of the Narragansett Church, pp. 139, 143.
5. Newport Records.

She married Judge James Helme, of South Kingstown, and died March 22, 1764, in her forty-sixth year. See Helme family, post. Mrs. Esther Powell died a widow, October 20, 1746, aged sixty-nine years, and was buried in the Congregational burying ground at Tower Hill.

Marie, another daughter of Gabriel Bernon, married Gabriel Tourtellot. See Tourtellot family, post.

Sarah, another daughter, married Benjamin Whipple, November 11, 1722.

Mr. Bernon's eldest son Gabriel and four daughters, children by his first wife, all came with him to America. This son died, unmarried, in early manhood by a shipwreck at the mouth of Narragansett Bay. In his will, dated February 16, 1727-8, proved in Providence, February 10, 1735-6, and there recorded, he mentions his former wife, Esther, his children, Mary Tourtellot, Esther Powell, Sarah Whipple, and Jane Coddington, and four small children by his present wife, Mary, viz. : Gabriel, Susanne, Mary, and Eve : also his son-in law, Benjamin Whipple. Of their latter children, Gabriel died young.

Susanne, born 1716, married Joseph, son of William Crawford, August 23, 1734.

Mary Bernon, born April 1, 1719 ; died October 1, 1789 ; married Gideon Crawford, son of William Crawford. He was born January 29, 1709 ; died 1792. Their daughter Sarah was the first wife of Capt. Zachariah Allen. Eve Bernon died unmarried.

The location of Bernon's dwelling house in Providence is perfectly well known.[1] It was on the lot of the original "Roger Williams Spring," on the west side of North Main street, and next north of his great grandson, Gov. Philip Allen's house.

1. Knowles's Life of Roger Williams, p. 431.

Almost directly opposite Bernon's house was the dwelling of Roger Williams, next to which, though at a later day, was King's Church, now St. John's.

G. Bernon House Lot.	W.+E. King's Church. Now St. John's.
	Church Street.
Roger Williams Spring. O	Roger Williams Lot.
	Howland Street.
Gov. Philip Allen's.	North Main Street.

At the age of eighty, Mr. Bernon embarked for Europe. and while in London, was presented at Court.

He died in Providence, R. I., February 21, 1736, aged 92 years, and was buried beneath St. John's Church, which owed its origin to him,[1] and in which a bronze tablet is erected to his memory. An obituary notice of him was published in Boston. He was a gentleman by birth and estate, and in leaving his native land the greater part of his estate was necessarily left behind him ; he was a courteous, honest, kindly gentleman, behaving himself as a zealous professor of the Protestant religion and dying in the faith and hope of a Redeemer, and with the inward assurance of salvation ; leaving a good name among all his acquaintances, and by his upright life giving evidence of the power of Christianity in sustaining him through his great sufferings

1. Arnold, vol. 2, p. 75.

in leaving his country and a great estate that he might worship God according to his conscience. A great concourse of people attended his funeral, and listened to an agreeable and eloquent sermon from Psalm 39 : 4, preached by the Rev. Mr. Brown.

The family of Bernon is registered in the "Historical and Genealogical Dictionary of the families of ancient Poitou," and it is stated there that the name has been known and celebrated since the "earliest ages of the French monarchy."

Numerous articles of value preserved among his descendants, go to show the wealth and social standing of Mr. Bernon.

For some of the numerous descendants of Bernon, see the families of Crawford, Allen, Tourtellot, Helme and Carpenter, post.

As the name of Carré is found in the Bernon genealogy it is very probable that Rev. Ezekiel Carré was a relative of Gabriel Bernon.

THE TOURTELLOT FAMILY.

We find on the Frenchtown plat the name of Abraum Tourtellot. He must, therefore, have been in this country in November, 1686.[1] He was engaged in mercantile pursuits, in partnership with his brother Benjamin, who died on a voyage from London to Boston, September 25, 1687, and Abraum was administrator of his brother's estate, the inventory of which would show a considerable trade. He lived at Roxbury, and by his wife, Mary, had two children, Gabriel, born September 24, 1694, and Esther, born June 12, 1696.

The tradition in the Rhode Island family is that they are descended from Gabriel Tourtellot, who was born at Bordeaux, and who married Marie, daughter of Gabriel Bernon, with whom he came over from Rochelle. Bernon's will, dated February 16, 1727–8, proved in Providence, February 10, 1735–6, mentions Mary Tourtellot among his children.

They, Gabriel and Mary, had three children, two sons and a daughter. He lived at Newport, and sailed from there, as master of a vessel, and was with his eldest son, (christian name unknown), lost at sea. The daughter married ———— Harding. Abram, the other son, settled in Gloucester, and was a large land owner there. His mother lived with him in Gloucester and died there. He married Lydia Ballard. Their children were :

First, Mary, born March 20, 1721 ; married ———— Mitchell. Second and third, Lydia and Esther, twins, born January 24, 1723; Lydia married Thomas Knowlton. Esther married Samuel Dunn. Fourth, Abram, born Feb-

---

1. Savage's Genealogical Dictionary, vol. 4, p. 315.

ruary 27, 1725; married ———— Harris, and settled in
Thomson, Connecticut. Fifth, Jonathan, born September
15, 1728; married ———— Williams, and settled in Scituate,
R. I. Sixth, Benjamin, born November 30, 1730; married
———— Ballard, and settled in Vermont. Seventh, Sarah,
married John Inman.

Abram, son of Gabriel, married, second, January 29,
1743, Hannah Corps, a widow, whose maiden name was
Case. They had five children :

1. Stephen, died young, of small pox.

2. William, married Phebe Whitman, of Providence,
and settled in Gloucester. Had eleven children: *a.* Mary.
b. Hannah. *c.* William, married Lydia Eddy; children:
Cyrus, Amasa R., now living, Abradia, John and Lydia. *d.*
Barbary. *e.* Nancy. *f.* Sarah. *g* and *h.* Hope and Mercy.
i. Whitman. *j.* Amey. *k.* Abram.

3. Jesse, married ———— Angell; setted in Mendon,
Massachusetts ; ten children.

4. Daniel, married Urana Keech, and lived and died in
Gloucester. By his first wife, he had three children: *a.*
Jesse, who was Judge of the Court of Common Pleas. He
married ———— Steere. They had twelve children; among
them was my old friend and schoolmate, Jesse S. Tourtellot. *b.* Jeremiah. *c.* Dorcas, who married Captain ———— —
Aborn, of Pawtuxet. Their son Robert lives in New York.

5. Anna, married first,———— Jones ; no children; second, Ebenezer White, who had six children: *a.* Nancy. *b.*
Esther. *c.* Nabby. *d.* Sally. *e.* Frances and *f.* Mary,
who was the second wife of her cousin Jesse, and he was her
second husband.

Abram, the son of Gabriel, married for his third wife,
———— Williams. No children.

CRAWFORD AND ALLEN FAMILIES.

Gideon Crawford emigrated from Lanark in Scotland, and settled in Providence about 1670. He married Freelove, daughter of Arthur Fenner, 1687; he died 1702; his grandson, Joseph, born 1712, married, 1734, Susanne, daughter of Gabriel Bernon. Their children were: First, Sarah; second, Joseph; third, Freelove, married John Jenckes; fourth, Susanne, married Samuel Nightingale; fifth, Mary, married Dr. Amos Throop; sixth, Candace, second wife of Capt. Zachariah Allen; seventh, Esther; eighth, Lydia; ninth, Anne, born in 1759; married Capt. Zachariah Allen, (third wife). She died in 1808. He died in 1801.

The children of Capt. Zachariah Allen and his third wife, were:

1.   Zachariah, died young.

2.   Lydia, born in 1782, married, in 1804, Sullivan Dorr, of Boston. She died in 1859. He died in 1853.

3.   Ann, died unmarried in 1859.

4.   Philip, B. U. 1803, married, in 1814, Phebe, daughter of Benjamin Aborn. He was Governor of the State, and Senator in Congress. He died in 1865. Mrs. Allen died in 1864.

5.   Candace, died in 1860, unmarried.

6.   Zachariah, born September 15, 1795. B. U. 1813. Married, May 1, 1817, Eliza Harriet Arnold, daughter of Welcome Arnold. She died August 30, 1873, aged 76. Mr. Allen received the degree of LL. D. from Brown University in 1851.

7.   Crawford, B. U., 1815, married, June 5, 1838, Sarah Senter, daughter of Rev. Nathan B. Crocker, D. D. He died April 22, 1872, aged 74.

HELME AND CARPENTER FAMILIES.

Rowse Helme, died 1712; his will is on record in Kingstown; his son, Rowse, married Sarah Niles, and died 1751. His children were: First, James, see post; second, Sands, died 1738; third, Rowse; fourth, Nathaniel; fifth, Benedict; sixth, Simeon; seventh, Benedict; eighth, Silas; ninth, Sarah; tenth, ———; eleventh, Oliver; twelfth, Samuel.

James Helme, born 1710; married Esther Powell, granddaughter of Gabriel Bernon, in 1738. Mr. Helme was elected Chief Justice of the Supreme Court, in 1767, and was a Judge of that Court for many years, and held other important offices. Their children were: First, Esther, born 1740, married Capt. Francis Carpenter, 1767 ; their son was Willett Carpenter, lately deceased; second, Powell, died 1780, single; third, Rowse J., who was an attorney at law, an account of him is given in Updike's Memoirs of the Rhode Island Bar ; fourth, Sarah ; fifth, Elizabeth; sixth, James, see post ; seventh, Adam, died unmarried; eighth, Samuel, born 1755, for many years Clerk of the Court in Washington county. His son, Powell, married Elizabeth Kenyon, was for many years clerk of the Supreme Court in Washington county, and Town Clerk of South Kingstown, and died October 20, 1861; ninth, Sarah; tenth, Gabriel, died single; eleventh, Nathaniel.

James Helme, son of Judge James, was born 1749-50, married Sarah Clarke, 1777 ; he died 1824, in South Kingstown. Their children were: First, James, who had children : *a.* James, now living at Woonsocket, married Elmira Allen, of Franklin, Massachusetts.

b. Sarah, married George Rickard, of Providence. They had seven children, of whom four are now living : 1. Sarah ;

2. James H., married Abby S. Weld of Woonsocket; 3. George Silas, married Penina Jackson, of Woonsocket; 4. Elizabeth Estelle.

c.   Mercy P., married James B. Ayres, of Yates county, New York. They had two children : 1.   Martha Wanton, married, 1st, Sanford W. Kress, of Yates county ; 2nd, Jacob Tremper.

d.   Jonathan Perry, married Mary, daughter of William James, of Providence. Had three children, only one now living, Anna P., married Leonard O. Smith, of Franklin, Connecticut, and is now living in Philadelphia.

e.   Adam Helme, married Ann Cory, living in South Kingstown. Children :   Mary E. ;   Hittie Ann ;   Adam Powell.

The other children of James, son of Judge James, were : Second, John, who married Susan, daughter of Elisha R. Gardner, and left two daughters : Mary, who married John Wilbur, of Fall River ; Ann, who married Thomas Nason, of Woonsocket.   After Mr. Helme's death, his widow married Rev. Israel Washburn, a Methodist clergyman. He died at Middleboro', Massachusetts, in 1864.

Third, Bernon, for many years clerk of the Court of Common Pleas in Providence County, died 1826 ; married Elizabeth Olney, 1811.   Had two children ; James Powell, who died 1825, aged eight years ; and Mary, who died single.

Fourth, Nathaniel, B. U. 1819 ; died 1822, unmarried. Was an excellent classical scholar, and for several years Instructor in the classical school at Little Rest, now Kingston.

Willett Carpenter, before named, married Elizabeth, daughter of Joseph Case and sister of the late Dr. Benjamin W. Case, of Newport.   He inherited the large estate on Boston Neck, which had belonged to the Willetts and owned it at the time of his death.   His children were :

Howell H., and Rev. James H. Carpenter, of Wakefield, a clergyman of the Episcopal Church.   On the Willett farm was the residence of Theophilus Whale or Whaley, supposed to be one of the regicide judges.[1]

1. For full account of the Willett family see Stiles' History of the judges; Thomson's History of Long Island, and Updike's History of the Narragansett Church.

THE GANEAUX FAMILY.

Francis Ganeaux came from Guernsey and settled at New Rochelle, where he died at the age of 103. The name was soon Englished into Gano. Stephen, son of Francis, had several children, of whom Daniel married Sarah, daughter of Nathaniel Britton, of Staten Island, and removed to Hopewell, New Jersey. Their children were: First, Daniel ; Second, Jane ; third, Stephen, died young : fourth, Susanna ; fifth, Rev. John Gano, born at Hopewell, July 22, 1777, ordained in 1754. He lived for some time at Frankfort, Kentucky, and died August 10, 1804. He married Sarah, daughter of John Stiles. Children: *a.* John, died in 1764. *b.* Daniel, born November 11, 1758. *c.* Peggy, born in 1760. *d.* Rev. Stephen, born December 25, 1762 ; settled over the First Baptist Church, in Providence, in 1792. *e.* Sarah, born February 4, 1764. *f.* John S., born in 1766. *g.* Isaac Eaton. *h.* Richard Montgomery. *i.* Susanna. *k.* William.

Sixth, Nathaniel; seventh, David; eighth, Sarah.[1]

Rev. Dr. Stephen Gano was thrice married, first to Cornelia Vavasour, October 25, 1782. Of their children, Cornelia V. married Rev. John Holroyd. Margaret H. married Rev. David Benedict, well known as the author of the History of the Baptists.

Second, married Mary Talmadge, August 4, 1789. Of their children, Sally S. married Rev. Peter Ludlow. Maria T. married Rev. Henry Jackson. Clarissa A. married, first, Newton Robbins, and second, James Ludlow.

Third, married Mary Brown, July 18, 1799. Their only child, Eliza Brown, married Joseph Rogers.

[1]. Benedict's History of the Baptists, vol. 1, pp. 485, 550, and vol. 2, p. 306. Memoir of Rev. John Gano, New York, 1806.

MARCHANT FAMILY.

The tradition of this family, as given me by the late Judge William Marchant, is that three brothers came over from Bayonne, in the time of the persecution, one of whom settled at Cape Cod, one at Barnstable and one at Martha's Vineyard, from which latter place Capt. Huxford Marchant, a sea captain, removed to Newport. His son, Henry, was educated for the bar and began the practice of the law in Newport, in which he attained great eminence. He was for several years a member of the first Continental Congress, and was one of those who signed the Articles of Confederation when adopted. He was Attorney General of the State. Like many others attached to the new government, he had to leave Newport while it was in the possession of the British. He purchased a farm in South Kingstown and lived there for a time.[1] He received the degree of LL. D. from Yale College in 1792, and died in 1796, at which time he held the office of United States District Judge.

His son, William Marchant, graduated at Yale, 1792. He resided for a time in Newport and afterwards in South Kingstown, where he died. He held the offices of Judge of the Supreme Court, the Chief Justice of the Court of Common Pleas, and member of the State Senate. He died January 21, 1857, aged eighty-two years. His son Henry was for a long time a manufacturer in Pawtucket and died in May, 1865. William, son of Judge William, is now living on the homestead farm in South Kingstown.

1. See an account of his life in Updike's Memoirs of the Rhode Island Bar.

TARGE FAMILY.

On the plat the name of this family is spelled Targé. In the old deeds and wills of the family in North Kingstown it is generally spelled Tourgée. After the breaking up of the French settlement the family remained in North Kingstown, but just over the Greenwich line in the immediate neighborhood of the proposed settlement. It seems from the plat that a father and son were among the settlers. The tradition as preserved in the family, gives the names of Peter and three sons: Peter, John and Philip. Professor Tourgée of the Boston Conservatory of Music, gives me the following, obtained from the records at Wickford. Children of Peter: First, Thomas, born December, 1722; second, Philip, born October, 1724; third, Elizabeth, born 1728; fourth, Peter, born February, 1733; fifth, John, December, 1735.

John died 1812. His son Jeremiah, born December, 1778 and died 1867. His son, Ebenezer, born in Warwick, 1809, died October, 1878, was father of Professor Eben Tourgée, of Boston.

THE LUCAS FAMILY.

This family was of French descent, and was connected with the Hillhouse and Brenton families, and in Narragansett with Matthew Robinson.[1] Augustus Lucas, the first emigrant, married Marie Lefebvre, daughter of Daniel Lefebvre, of Garhere, January 6, 1696, at St. Malo, in Bretagne. She died February 12, 1698, at Newport. He married, second, at Bristol, Barsheba Elliot, September 21, 1704. Their daughter, Barsheba, was born August 27, 1708, and died, the wife of Matthew Robinson, at Kingston, December 21, 1775.

1. Potter's Early History of Narragansett, p. 296, and Updike's Episcopal Church in Narragansett, pp. 280, 505, 506, and the notices of Matthew Robinson and Augustus Johnson in Updike's Memoirs of Rhode Island Bar.

THE JERAULD FAMILY.

In 1742 Dr. Dutee Jerauld, then about thirty years old, came from Medfield, Massachusetts, and settled in East Greenwich, and died in July, 1813, aged 91. His parents were Huguenot refugees. His father was a physician. One of his daughters married Samuel Pearce. Their son, Hon. Dutee J. Pearce, resided in Newport, and was a very able lawyer, Attorney General of the State, member of Congress for twelve years, and acquired considerable influence there. See Dr. Greene's History of East Greenwich, and Dr. Par sons' Sketches of Rhode Island Physicians.

THE GINNADO FAMILY.

Lewis Ginnado emigrated from France and married in Newport. He died in Exeter, Rhode Island, near Chapman's Mills, May 23, 1795, aged 79. His wife, Sarah, died in 1801. His daughter, Esther, married Gideon Freeborn. Daniel, his son, lived and died near Mumford's Mills. A lot of land there is still known by his name.

Daniel Ginnado's will was proved in South Kingstown, in February, 1816. In it he mentions his children, Samuel H., Lewis, Daniel, Joseph D., Susanna Sherman, Dorcas H., and Peggy.

The will of Daniel Ginnado, 2nd, was dated December, 1817, and proved in South Kingstown, January, 1818. He mentions his wife, Sally G. Ginnado, son, Samuel Slocum Ginnado, and nephews, Daniel and Alfred.

CLOSING NOTE.

Besides the families of whom we have given some account above, there are other families of French descent: The Levalleys, in Warwick; Jacques, Jaquais, Jacowaise; Le Baron; Geoffroy; Tarbox; Bardine, sometimes English from Bourdillé.[1] Andrew Nichols emigrated from Ireland, and married a French wife of the name of Petrel, and the late John T. Nichols, Sr., of Kingston, was their grandson. Louis Alaire, whose name is on the Frenchtown plat, was probably a relative of Bernon's.[2]

Of the Frenchtown settlers, the following, probably, went South: Collin, Jouet, Moize Lebrun, Legendre, St. Julien, and Legaré.[3]

For the documents from the British State Paper Office, including the map, we were indebted to the courtesy of Gen. Schenck, while minister at the Court of St. James. A reduced copy of this is prefixed. The other plat is reduced from the old plat of East Greenwich, and gives the lots as they were held by the settlers under the Rhode Island title.

We are indebted to several ladies and gentlemen for assistance and contributions; and more especially to Sidney S. Rider, for the great pains he has taken in contributing information and in making the statements, dates, etc., exact. Still, no doubt, errors will be found, as for instance, on page 61 it is related that a company of French settled at Chatham Four Corners, in New York: the word French is an error for Friends, and was not discovered in time to be corrected; and again on page 19, the name Legree should have been Legaré.

1. Massachusetts Historical Collections, volume 22, page 81.
2. Bernon Family, and also Savage's Genealogical Dictionary.
3. Mrs. Lee's Huguenots in France and America, volume 2.

www.ingramcontent.com/pod-product-compliance
Lightning Source LLC
Chambersburg PA
CBHW020038030726
47499CB00007B/2490